W9-AQZ-229

CONTAGION

THE TOXIC CITY TRILOGY

LONDON EYE

REAPER'S LEGACY

CONTAGION

TIM LEBBON

CONTAGION

Published 2013 by Pyr®, an imprint of Prometheus Books

Jacket design by Nicole Sommer-Lecht

Inquiries should be addressed to

Pyr
59 John Glenn Drive
Amherst, New York 14228–2119
VOICE: 716–691–0133
FAX: 716–691–0137
WWW.PYRSF.COM

17 16 15 14 13   5 4 3 2 1

Library of Congress Cataloging-in-Publication Data

Lebbon, Tim.
Contagion / By Tim Lebbon.
pages cm. — (Toxic City ; Book Three)
ISBN 978-1-61614-821-8 (hardcover) — ISBN 978-1-61614-822-5 (ebook)
1. Terrorism—Fiction. 2. London (England)—Fiction. I. Title.

PS3612.E245C66 2013
813'.6—dc23

2013024869

Printed in the United States of America

This one's for Dan the Man.

CHAPTER ONE
SEVENTEEN

Jack viewed the endless stars, the incredible depth of space, and the sense of eternity surrounding him, but he was not afraid. He belonged in this universe deep inside himself. With effort, he would flex it to his will.

He moved quickly, flitting from star to star and orbiting briefly as he considered the gifts they might bestow upon him. Some he recognised, because he had used them before. Others were mysterious, massive and cold, closed to him for now. He did not like such mystery, but now was not the time to probe them.

A few were ready to reveal themselves, and it was these he sought.

"Get a bloody move on!"

Jack blinked away the voice, frustrated. *Leave me alone!* He drifted through those interior constellations, closing on one blue star that seemed to pulse each time he blinked. The blueness belied its deep, hot heart, and he plummeted, delving inside and surrounding himself with its wonder.

"For shit's sake, Jack!"

Sparky, shut up! he thought. He wanted to speak, but feared that might break his concentration. When he rose, he had to drag their salvation with him.

He felt a hand grasp his arm and pull him down, and as he struck the hard ground, gunshots echoed across the vastness of his perception.

Okay, now, here we go, I'm ready to—

In the distance, something red. It was unlike anything he had seen before. It seemed to swell, as if reacting to his noticing it. A deep, bloody red object, too large for a star, larger than many constellations, and seeing it brought him suddenly, terrifyingly close. The red thing was covered with swirling storms and tumultuous explosions, and more than anything it showed him the sheer scale of this inner world he had discovered.

No, not discovered. Been given. Because this had been thrust upon him, and any sense he had of control was surely balanced on a knife-edge.

"Jack, we've got about three seconds until—"

One . . .

Jack circled the red object, and it throbbed. Each pulse matched the beating of his heart.

Two . . .

He pulled away, rising up and out of himself. The red giant watched.

Three . . .

And as he emerged into the chaos of the toxic city of London once more, he realised something awful.

That red thing within him was alive.

Gunfire stitched the wall above their heads. Smashed brick rained down on them, some shattered shards kissing across Jack's forearm. Blood weeped. It made him shiver.

Sparky was staring at him, depending on him. Behind him, Jenna was sheltering Rhali with her own body, the girl still weak and confused from her terrible incarceration at Camp H.

They were trapped beneath an old brick railway arch, pinned down by three Choppers who had almost literally driven into them. As he and his friends had run for cover, Jack had barely had time to be glad that his sister and mother were already out of London. And then the gunfire had begun. There was no demand that they surrender, no negotiation. These Choppers had been told to shoot on sight and were glad to do so.

With each fusillade of bullets they'd been forced deeper beneath the arch as the Choppers ventured closer, their angle of fire changing. Behind them, heavy steel gates and gratings cut off any hope of retreat. The space beneath the archway smelled of damp, piss, and hopelessness.

But Jack was far from helpless.

He stood, took in one deep breath, and shouted.

His voice bore weight and heat. He pushed the power that had changed his father into the monster called Reaper, and the air before him blurred with the terrible energies unleashed. Combined with the heat of the new talent he had just touched, the destruction was awful. Loosened bricks were smashed from the high arch's outer curve, shattering in the air and peppering the buildings across the street with molten shrapnel. Windows burst inward, glass shards melted, doors smashed open, and several vehicles resting on flat tyres were flipped onto their sides and crushed against the buildings—a pub, a betting shop, several boarded-up homes. Window frames ignited. Car tyres flowed.

Jack knew there were three Choppers hiding behind these vehicles, but he felt very little remorse. Not then. That, and the guilt, would come later.

As his incredible shout faded, its echoes were replaced by the musical tinkle of falling glass and the patter of brick fragments. A Mercedes that had been crushed against the pub's front wall tilted, creaked, then fell back onto its tyres with a dull crash. Its heated metal ticked and groaned as it cooled. A shape slid down the wall behind it, leaving a dark smear against the brickwork. Night hid the full scene from Jack, and for that he was glad.

"Bloody hell," Sparky said.

"Keep down," Jenna said. She shifted forward, signalling to Rhali that she should stay back as far as she could.

"Jenna, careful!" Jack said. She went to her knees to look out into the dark street. There was moonlight, and a starscape that made Jack feel uncomfortable. And he knew also that there were night scopes and heat detection equipment, and that any Choppers watching would not have been shocked into immobility at his display of power. His father's use of it had killed many of their comrades, after all.

"I think they're down," Jenna said.

Down. She could have said dead, Jack thought. *Or crushed, or smeared across the road. But instead she tells me that they're down.* He could have searched for a power and sensed outwards, perhaps, looking for signs of pain or indications of life. But right then he had no wish to revisit that constellation of potential still growing inside him. Not when that red thing was there as well.

"Then let's get the hell out of here," he said. "We need to hide low 'til daylight, plan what to do."

"Finding Lucy-Anne is what we do!" Sparky said.

"Yeah," Jack said. He looked at Rhali and smiled. She did not smile back. He wondered what damage she must have suffered, physically and mentally, at the hands of the Choppers and their sick leader, Miller. Perhaps soon he would ask. "But first we've gotta find somewhere to rest. We can't run into another Chopper patrol, not now. They're out for revenge for what's happened to their mates, and . . ."

"And you're tired," Jenna finished for him.

"Yeah. Exhausted."

"Pussy," Sparky said.

Jack smacked him playfully across the shoulder, and they hurried quickly along the street. He did not once look back. But that could not stop him from thinking of the people he had just killed.

During his brief time in London he had already witnessed so much violent death. One death was too many for someone of his age, but he had seen many more than that—Choppers killed by Reaper, and Fleeter, and other Superiors in their ongoing game of cat and mouse in the remains of London; Irregulars caught in the crossfire; and the shelved and jarred remnants in Camp H, grim evidence of Miller's inhuman vivisection of the Doomsday survivors.

But he had never killed. The very idea of it was sickening to him, and it was a line he had never dreamt of crossing. Now, he had. Minutes before, three people with memories and loves, lives and ambitions, fears and desires, had been alive in this world, and now because of him they were no more. They had ceased to be, and the consequences of their deaths would ripple outward beyond London, touching wives and husbands, children and parents. Jack had become a harbinger of tears.

Perhaps I'm like him now, he thought, picturing the man who had been his father. And yet Reaper was a monster, acting only upon his own selfish needs. Killing was a pleasure to him, and Jack had witnessed him delighting in it more than once.

Jack was different. He was trying his very best to save London, and everyone left alive in that once-great place.

He had to insist upon that—he was *different*.

The deaths weighing heavily, he led his friends deeper into the doomed city.

Lucy-Anne knows that she is dreaming. But this time she is a passive observer, and whatever strange power drives her dreams is cruel. It keeps her prisoner, frozen into immobility, eyes open, able only to watch as Rook falls again and again, trying to grab her and scratching three trails across the back of her hand with his nails. They will scar, if she lives long enough. Even without these nightmares, she will have a reminder.

She struggles to cry out a warning to him. But each time she does so it's too late, and he is already down in the pit. She hears his screams of terror and then agony again and again. The dreams give her that. *I'm sorry*, she thinks, but by then Rook is already falling once more.

She tries to wake, but in this dream she cannot pinch herself. *Perhaps this is hell*, she thinks. Rook falls again.

Pain cuts in across the back of her hand, a cruel heat. Lucy-Anne gasps, and then—

—the gasp came again, echoing back at her from the small room where she had taken refuge. It was a lonely sound, yet it made her feel safe. She was alone here, as she had been when she'd crawled this way, blood dribbling from the wound on her scalp, emptiness around her where Rook and his birds should have been. The scrapes across the back of her hand were already rough with dried blood.

Awake in the darkness, Lucy-Anne felt the warm comfort of fresh tears. She'd believed that she had saved Rook, dreaming away his fall into the pit and death at the jaws of the worm-thing. But fate had found him at last. Perhaps that was simply how it worked.

She sat with her back against the damp wall and looked around the dark room. Furniture hunkered, shadows frozen. Pictures on the walls reflected weak moonlight filtering through the net curtains. Close to the edge of Hampstead Heath, the house smelled like time stood still. She felt the same way, floating in that strange time between sleep and wakefulness when dreams still intruded, and reality was reforming around her. The more of the real world that flooded in, the more wretched she felt, because it was not only Rook who was dead.

"Andrew, my sweet brother," she whispered, and then she heard a sound. She froze, holding her breath and her tears, head tilted. She started breathing out slowly, aiding her hearing, and then it came again—something in the next room, brushing against a wall. She stood, pain pounding through her skull. If she had to run, the front door was out in the hallway opposite the room where the sound originated. She could turn the other way, maybe, run towards the rear of the house, but she had not checked back there when she'd crawled in. She'd barely looked anywhere.

She stood as motionless and silent as could be, and something dropped into the doorway.

A rook. She knew it instantly, because she had been so close to them over the past couple of days. Her fear evaporated. She held her breath and her heart hammered as she listened for footsteps behind the bird. *He'll saunter in now and smile at me, shrug when I ask what happened, and I'll dream us together forever*.

But there were no footsteps. And after looking at her for a few seconds the rook skipped out of sight. She darted after it, reaching the corridor just in time to see it hop into the other room, and reaching the doorway to that room in time to see it take flight through a broken window pane. By the time she stood at the window the bird was gone. The darkness had swallowed it, just as it had the creature's master.

Awake now, welcoming the pain from her bruised scalp and scratched hand, Lucy-Anne looked north towards the shadowy landscape of Hampstead Heath.

I'm told that there is a bomb, Nomad had told her and Rook. *A nuclear bomb*. She'd looked directly at Lucy-Anne as she spoke, because both of them had known that anyway. They had seen it in their dreams. *The people of the north—the ones you see as monsters—they know also. They have* sensed *it. And they're not as monstrous as they seem*. Lucy-Anne had been unable to talk, taken as she was with the memory of those terrible dreams—conflagration, destruction, the cloud that London would become. But Rook had asked her more. *I don't know where or when*, had been Nomad's response, and Rook had grown angry, even though he feared her. With one more glance at Lucy-Anne, the mysterious woman had left.

"All of this, gone," Lucy-Anne whispered. She expected no reply from the city, but in the distance a long, lonely cry rose up, part animal, part human. She had no wish to know what might make such a sound.

She closed her eyes and took a deep breath, shrugging off dreams and memories and those crippling visions that seemed to pin her to unreality. This was real. She was here, alone, with a message to tell, and with friends to find again. She'd abandoned Jack, Jenna and Sparky, and Jack's sweet sister Emily, when she had first discovered the truth about her dead parents. Plenty had changed since then—in her, and around her—but she found some shred of comfort in the realisation that some things never change.

Friendship, for instance.

She had been running south for her friends when she'd tripped and banged her head. Now, she took a few moments to root through the house she had sheltered in, searching for useful things. She found a leather jacket that had seen better days, two tins of food in the kitchen that might still be edible, and a carving knife that she slipped into her belt.

Out in the street she turned south and started to jog, and doing something positive made her feel safer.

Behind her, a shape parted from shadows and followed.

In the cool night, Nomad sat in the shattered thirteenth floor window of an office block, looking out across a city that should never be dark. Starlight silvered the buildings and roads, the tree canopies of parks, and the uneven contours of car parks filled with vehicles that would never move again. Night neutralised colour, and hers was a grey London tonight. Out there she could still sense her boy Jack, struggling with the changes she had planted within him whilst attempting to save his family. She could sense Lucy-Anne, that girl who had been special even before Doomsday. And she wanted to protect them both.

That was why she was here. High, quiet, apart from the violence that sometimes ruled the streets down below, she breathed in the scents of her city. The pain still nestled in her chest, and she knew what that meant. Many across London suffered the same sickness. But pain was fleeting and temporary. Even though she bled from her nose when she reached outward, and her head throbbed blindingly when she listened, she could not let it matter.

Beyond the pain she heard time itself.

It grumbled in the settling of a thousand old brick foundations, and many more newer beds of concrete. It whispered in the imperceptible flow of old glass, gravity urging it slowly, so slowly down. It sang in the straining growth of countless trees, shrubs, flowers and grasses, and murmured stiffly in other plants' demise. Time's flow swept the city forward and drove the clogged Thames, corroding, worrying at bridge supports and the concrete banks built up to stop the flooding that would inevitably occur one day. Every breath was a moment further away from time's beginning, and every footfall was one step closer to the end. She flowed with it for a while, enjoying being in tune with not only nature itself, but the inscrutable time that moved it ever-onward. The pains became dulled with time's promise that pain would always end. Then she focussed, listening and sensing for those ways in which humanity made itself aware.

In the distance, the *tick-tick* of a wrist watch on someone still living. Further afield, the heavier clicks of a wall clock passing each second. She heard and disregarded countless sounds, senses, feelings, passing them by in her search for the one that mattered. When she found it, its nature and purpose were obvious.

It counted backwards.

To the south, in a locked place so well shielded from outside that the air inside must smell of almost two years ago, the city's destruction sat in an object barely the size of a suitcase.

Seventeen hours, thirteen minutes, twenty-eight seconds . . .

The pains kicked in again, possessing her bones and blood and seeming to melt away her whole body as if caught in a terrible blast. She shivered, and groaned.

"Oh, no," Nomad muttered. More words stolen by the breeze. They added to the utterances of desperation and hopelessness made since Doomsday and still echoing from old brick and stone, and Nomad rested onto her back as she gratefully withdrew into herself again.

Seventeen hours . . .

CHAPTER TWO SIXTEEN

Jack could not sleep. Dawn smeared London's jagged horizon, its palette slowly illuminating the crossroads in front of the furniture store. He lay on a double bed deep in the shop, hands behind his head, watching through the dusty shop front as the West Kensington street scene was revealed. Several cars had burned, and sometime since Doomsday they had been shoved onto a pavement across the road, leaving a swathe of melted, blackened tarmac.

Every time he blinked, he wondered at the names of the three men or women he had just killed.

Someone sat on the bed beside him. Rhali. Jack shoved down his self-pity. She might not have killed, but she had been through so much more than him.

"The others are asleep," she said. Her accent was smooth and calming, her voice soft.

"Sparky and Jenna," Jack said.

"Yes. They told me their names. They're within the chairs." At the rear of the shop they'd found a circle of fifteen luxury armchairs, obviously formed since Doomsday. Dust patterns showed that they had not been used for some time. Jenna had muttered something about a protective circle, and for some reason she and Sparky felt safer there.

Rhali lay down beside Jack, lighter than she should have been, more fragile.

"How are you feeling?" Jack asked.

"I was about to ask the same."

"I'm okay," he said.

"They were trying to kill us." Her voice, still soft, now somehow lacked emotion. "They are *always* trying to kill us. If you hadn't done what you did, they would have come closer, and shot us, and left us there for the dogs and rats. Cats too, I've heard. Have you heard that? Cats are eating the dead."

"Never liked cats," Jack said. "Crafty. Always thought they'd eat us in the end."

Rhali breathed quickly, an almost-laugh. She drew closer to Jack and pulled at his left arm, lying on it, her side against his. There was nothing sexual about it at all. She needed contact, and they both took comfort from it.

"Sparky and Jenna have told me what's happening," she said. "I say let it burn. London is nothing now. Even the memories are fading. Have you smelled the air? It's almost clean. London should never smell like this."

"You were born here?"

"Peckham. Mum and Dad . . ." She trailed off, and he did not prompt her. Some kept their stories inside because they were too painful to tell.

"I don't want to save the city, I want to save the people."

"And your friend, Lucy-Anne."

"Yes, and her. She and I . . . we're good friends. Close." He remembered when he'd first met her, defiant and rebellious, and how she dyed her hair and wore clothes she thought might annoy or antagonise, and he felt a rush of love. It was deep and old, not passionate; the love for someone he had known for sixty years, not two. Doomsday had aged them all, and perhaps because they had both been through so much, they had earned the right to such affection.

"Some of them deserve to die," Rhali said. She fell silent, watching daylight dawn with Jack. He waited with her until she was ready to continue, and then pulled her closer when she did. She sounded so cold that he thought she could use some warmth.

"I'd met a boy called Jamie. Soon after everything went bad. He was nice, just as lost as me. We travelled to the south, intending to try to get out, and heard about what had happened to others doing the same. We decided to try anyway. But when we got close, we saw the bodies. They'd put them on display. And every one had . . . had . . . they'd taken their brains." She shivered, and Jack pulled her close. "There were a lot more people back then. Already I could sense something, though I was confused, didn't yet know what it was. Movement, drifting, like smoke in the night. Jamie and I waited there for a couple of weeks, and then they started bombing and burning. Making their exclusion zone around the city. There was smoke and fire for days. So we turned north again, and that's when they caught us."

Something moved out in the street, and Jack felt Rhali stiffen against him.

"Hey," he said. "It's just dogs." One big Labrador trotted along the street, and several more dogs followed. The pack was lean and strong, feral, displaying none of the playfulness of pets. Another sadness.

"They killed Jamie," Rhali said. "He struggled a bit, and they pushed him against a wall and shot him. Then they took me and asked me what I could do. I thought . . . I thought they were going to kill me too. I wanted them to. I swore and fought and scratched, and they hit me. Next thing I knew I was in the back of a truck, and he . . . Miller, that bastard, was sticking needles in me. Taking blood. I kicked him, and he jabbed me a few times just out of spite."

Jack imagined holding a gun to Miller's head. He'd done that just several hours previously, and Sparky had reminded him of who he was. *Now I've killed anyway*, Jack thought, and he wished Miller had been the first.

"What could Jamie do?" he asked.

"I never knew," Rhali said. "I'm not sure he did, either. He died right at the beginning."

"What a waste." Jack sat up and pulled her with him, and something made him hug her tight, both arms around her and holding her close. She hugged back, hard. There was a desperation there, and a need to hold and feel someone who was still human. So many people Jack had concerned himself with seemed to have left humanity behind—Miller, the Superiors. Reaper, who had once been his father. What a waste.

"Suppose I should have warned you he was a fast worker," Sparky said, jumping onto the bed, laughing. Rhali pulled away, and for the first time Jack heard her laugh. It was muffled by tears. He hadn't been aware that she was crying. He was surprised to find that he was, too. He was relieved at the interruption, but knew that he and Rhali would talk more. She had more to tell.

"You two okay?" Jenna asked. She appeared beside them carrying two cans of Coke. They'd found a stash out back, and though flat they were perfectly drinkable.

"Oh, just bloody dandy," Jack said. They all laughed then, and it was a release of tension. Jack wondered whether anyone or anything out in the streets heard, and right then, caution be damned, he hoped they did.

It might be the last laughter London ever heard.

Nomad had come here to see, but wished she hadn't.

The museum had been sealed against intrusion. Its lower windows were smashed, but no one had made it past the metal security grilles. She closed her eyes and opened three sets of doors, and her nose bled as she entered.

It was musty inside, and sparse. The reception area looked as new as the day it was built. Beyond, the main display hall was vast, and filled with the green and grey of war machines. They stood on plinths, on the floor surrounded by chain boundaries, and hung from the roof structure on strong cables. All of them were frozen in falsely peaceful poses, but each exuded violence. All built to destroy.

And there were traps everywhere.

Just inside the doors was a network of fine trip wires. Above, metal vats painted the same war-colours contained a mix of lethal compounds. Almost without thinking, Nomad knew what they could do. When tipped, their contents would mix and haze into a corrosive gas. Flesh would liquefy. Eyes would melt. Lungs would burn, and anyone in the area would die in suffocating agony.

There were pressure pads on the staircases. She probed further, and found the explosives they were linked to. Small charges—they didn't want to bring the building down—but enough to blow the legs off their intended victims, and perhaps gut them.

There were movement sensors everywhere, and even Nomad grew nervous, trying to lessen her movements as she breathed in the old air and tried to weather the pain. Each spread of sensors initiated different responses—she could smell poisons and gases, feel the slick coolness of guns against her palms, hear the echoes of explosions that would occur if she placed one foot wrong.

Her heart felt heavy and cumbersome, her blood slow and thick. *I'm not meant to die like this!* she thought, but she could not deny the sickness that using her talents made worse. She had seen it in others more and more recently, and now she had it herself. She supposed that was fair.

"Even if I get past everything . . ." she whispered, then held her breath in case she had missed microphones. Nothing exploded, nothing shot at her. The balance persisted, and she dwelled only briefly on the greater problem.

The bomb was locked inside a tank. She could sense its heat, and its terrible potential.

Even if I reach the bomb, how do I stop it? Sixteen hours, only sixteen, and whatever I do could trigger it. There will be safeguards, triggers, to avoid interference. If I look at it wrong, it might explode. If I breathe on it, touch it, attempt to move it . . .

Nomad was at a loss. London was hers, even now. But this building was no longer part of London. This was the fate that awaited her city, and to avoid it she had to think beyond the physical.

Filled with doubt, Nomad retraced her steps and left the building. And despite the pain and blood, and the confusion in her ever-more diseased mind, she was careful to seal the entrance doors once again.

"So, what's the plan?" Sparky asked. They'd retreated to the rear of the shop and now sat in the chair circle. It felt unaccountably safe, as if the empty chairs were actually occupied by guardian angels.

Jack looked around at his friends, old and new. It was strange how he felt he'd known Sparky and Jenna a lifetime, instead of just the two years since Doomsday, when being left on their own had drawn them together. But he supposed between then and now *was* a lifetime.

Sparky, with his spiky blond hair, broad shoulders, gruff attitude and caring heart. He'd lost his brother, but he was weathering the grief well. Jack liked to think their relationship helped. Jenna mourned her father, not dead, but taken from her because of his interest in London's fate. He was half the man he'd used to be. And now Rhali, thinner than she should be, bearing the weight of whatever tortures they had seen fit to subject her to, and yet still beautiful. Every time Jack looked at her his heart skipped a little. It was a feeling he'd never had with Lucy-Anne, and for now he tried not to analyse it too much. There were more urgent matters to deal with.

"Plan?" Jenna asked. "As if."

"Do what we have to," Jack said. "Spread the word about the bomb, find Lucy-Anne, get the hell out of London."

"Easy," Sparky said. "Piece of cake." He glanced at Rhali.

"We're assuming Miller wasn't lying about the bomb," Jenna said.

"We have to," Jack replied. "Big Bindy, he called it. And Breezer seemed pretty sure he was telling the truth."

"Breezer being completely trustworthy, of course," Sparky said.

"I heard them talking about Big Bindy," Rhali said. "I never figured out who or what it could be. But the Choppers I heard were scared of her. Or it."

"Makes sense," Jack said. "Miller and his cronies didn't really know all they were dealing with, even after all this time. They did their best to keep London contained, and that seemed to be working. But if they ever found something, or someone, that might have broken out—become a real threat to the rest of the country, for all they knew—they'd have some way of stopping that."

"So what's changed?" Sparky asked. He stood, hands held out. No one replied. "I don't mean why did Miller press the button. Reason is, he's a dick. Easy enough. What I mean is, how can anyone get out of London, even if we now have to?"

"Dunno," Jack said.

"I mean, they'll be even more determined to keep the Doomsday survivors trapped now, won't they?" Sparky asked.

"Yeah," Jenna said. "Make sure Big Bindy gets them all."

Sparky stared at Jack, waiting for him to respond. Jack felt uncomfortable beneath his friend's gaze, because he knew what Sparky was thinking. Perhaps what they were *all* thinking, including Rhali, who'd already had a glimpse at what Jack could do.

He skimmed the starscape inside, and that throbbing red giant was still there. Watching him. Waiting.

"I can't do anything," Jack said.

"What?" Sparky said. "*Nothing?*"

Jack shook his head. "I've thought about it. Looked. You've seen what I can do. There's other stuff, but I'm not certain of any of it yet. Some of what I've been able to do has been because I've been close to someone else doing it, like Reaper and his shout. Other stuff has come to me . . . sort of instinctively." He shrugged.

"Tell everyone," Sparky said. "That's what we need to do. Spread the word about the bomb, arrange a meeting place ready to break out of the city. Now that she's not working for them—" He'd nodded at Rhali, and she stood, angry.

"I've *never* worked for them!" she shouted. "Have you any idea what they did to me to make me tell them things? I'll tell you one day. Big, brave boy, I'll tell you."

"Hey . . ." Sparky said, and they could all see how sorry he was. "I didn't mean that. Really."

Rhali nodded, and even offered him a half-smile.

"And there's what Miller said," Jenna said softly. "About how using the powers has led to people getting sick."

"Yeah," Sparky said. "This is all so shit."

"So what's new," Jack said.

"I'm not sick," Rhali said. "Malnourished, yeah. And the drug they were giving me, whatever it is, it's got side effects you don't even wanna know about."

"Not everyone's ill," Jack said. "Not yet. But there are more and more. My mum was working as a healer in a hospital set up in a tube station, and she was seeing lots. No way to treat them. No cure, even from a healer."

"I guess all these powers are new," Jenna said. "And so's the disease."

"A cure is for later," Jack said. "Our priority now is finding Lucy-Anne and getting everyone out of London. I'll do whatever I can to make that happen."

"Or finding the bomb," Sparky said.

"You know how to disarm an atom bomb, dickhead?" Jack asked.

Sparky raised his eyebrows and slowly raised his middle finger at Jack. "Well, my young Padawan, I was only thinking—"

"Sure he does," Jenna said. "He's seen James Bond."

"But if we can find it and—"

"Stick it up his butt and jump in the Thames, float it into the North Sea," Jack said.

"Right then," Sparky said. He turned and stomped off, mock-offended. Jenna chuckled.

"Miller," Rhali said softly.

"He said he doesn't know where it is," Jack said.

"We don't need to know," she said. "Like you said, none of us could do anything about it even if we did. But that bastard Miller's the boss. He could call off his thugs, open a way out of London."

"But would he?" Jenna asked.

Rhali looked at Jack, one eyebrow raised. And Jack grinned.

"You're a genius, as well as pretty," he said, and Rhali glanced down at her feet, embarrassed.

"Hey, now, who's getting jiggy with it?" Sparky said.

"You could persuade him?" Jenna asked Jack.

"If not me, then I know a man who can."

"Yeah!" Sparky said. "That dude with Breezer. 'Drop your weapons,' and every Chopper in sight did it."

"Might work," Jenna said. "If we can find Miller, and if he isn't surrounded by a hundred Choppers, and if he's even still in the city."

"And if your father left him alive," Rhali said.

"He'll have left him alive," Jack said. "And he'd have made sure Miller couldn't leave. He was enjoying torturing him too much for that."

"So where is he?" Jenna asked.

"That's something else Breezer could help us with," Jack said. "So right now, he's the man to find."

"Right then," Jenna said after a few moments. "Clock's ticking."

"Yeah, and we don't even know how long's left." Sparky's tone was grim. It was daylight now, and Jack was already nervous about going out into the streets again. Ever since they had arrived, each dawn had brought a more vicious, brutal London to life.

As plans went, it seemed hazy at best. But it felt good to be doing something positive rather than sitting in the furniture shop, letting the weight of events crush him down. And as they left, Rhali's hand felt good in his.

Jenna and Sparky followed behind, comfortable in their closeness. A couple only for a matter of days, it seemed to Jack that they had been together forever. He loved them. They were his friends, and the idea of anything happening to them was horrible. *They will die*, he thought, an idea that often impinged upon him about the ones he loved. Sometimes he hated his sense of morbidity. *They'll die, we'll all die. But I want them to live first.*

None of them knew when the bomb was set to blow. The pressure of Big Bindy was all around them, and in their own ways they were all aware of it. Each step he took might have been his last. Every breath, each glance, every thought might be his final act in this world. Everything in the city seemed primed to accept the light, the heat, and then the blast that would bring its destruction. The silence seemed different from usual; a held breath rather than an absence. For now, everything mattered about the city and the people still alive within it. It was important. But one blast and the resulting vaporisation of everything he could see would make it unimportant. From one moment to the next London might cease to be, and all his worries would end.

But Jack wanted the worries. He wanted to persist, survive, and drive forward into the new world that Doomsday had seeded. It was too important to have all been for nothing.

They headed east, moving quickly but cautiously, listening for motors that might give away the presence of Choppers in the vicinity. They could not afford another confrontation. Jack had no wish to kill again, ever. But he knew he would if he had to.

"McDonald's!" Sparky said. The remains of the burger bar took up one street corner. Its windows had been smashed and a burnt-out car was crushed against the entrance doors, but adverts for cheap burgers were still hanging behind the shattered glass.

"You eat that shit?" Rhali asked.

"Hell, yeah!" Sparky said. "I could eat about ten of their cheese-burgers right now."

"And take ten days off your life."

"You don't look like a health food freak," Sparky said, and they all paused, a loaded silence.

Then Rhali burst out laughing, and the others joined in.

"Er, I didn't mean . . ." Sparky said, but Jenna slapped him playfully around the head.

"They'll be the first back in if we open London up again," Jack said. "Day one: four hundred McDonald's branches re-open in London."

"And I will live here in luxury," Sparky said.

They moved on. A group of dogs crossed their path several hundred yards along the street, and they paused until the pack had disappeared. Jenna looked at Jack, waiting for him to access a power to check the dogs had gone. He didn't.

Three people dashed from the cover of a Tube station entrance, looked their way, then ran along the street, hissing and clicking in what might have been a strange language. Again, Jenna looked to Jack, but he shook his head and waved them on.

He dipped in and out of the universe of potential he carried inside, and each time that pulsing, living red star stared back. It was as aware of him as he was of it, and it scared him. He did not like the fear. He wanted to know more, but to do that he would have to take back possession of his starscape.

Soon he would go deep and confront it, touch it, find out exactly what it was. Soon.

Rhali squeezed his hand. She stopped walking, and if he hadn't caught her she would have fallen. He was amazed at how feverish she felt, and her lightness shocked him afresh.

"What is it?" he asked tenderly.

"Something not normal," she said. "Sit me down. Let me . . ." She drifted off, her eyes rolled, and Jack eased her down to the pavement and leaned her against a shop front. It had used to sell wedding dresses, but now its window was home to a leathery corpse.

Jenna knelt beside her, and Sparky stood guard, scanning the street in either direction and glancing back at them to see what was happening.

"Is this how she does it?" Jenna asked.

"Don't know," Jack said.

"What's wrong with you, Jack?" It surprised him that Jenna would query his well-being while Rhali was like this. But then Jenna hardly knew this girl, and Jack was her friend. She'd sensed that he was troubled the evening before, and it must have been playing on her mind.

"Something," he said, touching his head. "In here. Something strange."

"To do with Nomad?"

"I think it's *all* to do with Nomad."

"So many," Rhali said. She squeezed Jack's hand tighter, then smiled weakly at him to let him know she was all right. Then she closed her eyes again. "It's all normal everywhere else . . . people moving around, cautious, smallish groups. Looking for food. Safety. But there's something so strange . . . big groups, all moving the same way. Fleeing something. Or heading for something else."

"Where?" Jack asked. He looked up at Sparky, who shrugged and held out his hands: *All clear here.*

"From the north," Rhali said. "There are dozens of them, perhaps hundreds. And they're all coming down from the north."

"Oh, shit me," Sparky said. "Guys, don't want to add to the crap quotient, but we have a guest."

Jack looked up, keeping hold of Rhali's hand. Jenna stood shoulder to shoulder with Sparky. And they all stared along the street at the woman walking towards them.

To Jack, Nomad looked different from before. Lessened, and weaker. But her eyes still blazed, and for an instant they reminded him of that glowing red star.

She paused when she was a dozen steps from them. She only had eyes for Jack.

"My boy," she said. "I've come to save you."

CHAPTER THREE FIFTEEN

Two of them had been with Jack the time she bestowed her gift upon him. The other was a stranger. But she did not care about those around him. It was Jack who mattered, Jack she had to help. Up to now he had managed to help himself, but this was something more. The bomb was unstoppable. And Jack was going the wrong way.

"My boy, I've come to save you."

Jack released the girl's hand. She was slumped against the shop facade, sick. Nomad thought perhaps she might never rise again, but right then she did not care. Jack came towards her, and already she could sense the staggering change in him.

"Oh, you're everything I wanted this to be," she whispered.

"You're bleeding." Jack was staring at her mouth, and Nomad lifted a hand to touch the blood dribbling from her nose. It tasted alien, as if it belonged to someone else. He asked, "You're sick too?"

"No." It shocked her that she should choose to lie. That was a purely human conceit, and she had removed herself from humanity.

"Yes," Jack said. "Just like all of them. So can you stop the bomb?"

"No, Jack," she said. The others came into focus around Jack now, and for the first time Nomad considered them as more than shadows. They stood together as if they were part of him.

"Why not? You're Nomad. All powerful, feared by everyone, and if you can do this to me, surely you can do anything!"

"I'm here to take you out," she said. "Just you. Out of London where you'll be safe when—"

"I'm not leaving without my friend."

Nomad glanced at the girl on the ground, the stocky boy, the other girl. "I'll take them, too," she said, not sure whether she was lying again.

"Not them. Our other friend. And everyone else. Will you really leave London to its fate after you caused all of this?"

"It's evolution," she said. "And you're the future."

"No," he said. "Help us if you can. Stop the bomb, warn everyone. Make it so everyone can leave."

"Fifteen hours." Nomad frowned, confused. "That's how long you have. But I'll never take you out by force, Jack. You have to *want* to be special, to be saved. I don't want you to doom yourself."

"You're too late for that," he said quietly. He was facing up to her and, though scared, so were his friends.

"I'll be watching you." Nomad searched inside, trying to grasp something that would change how things were. But Jack was his own boy. She had told the truth—she would not save him by force. He was as special as she was, and he had to *want* everything she had given him for it to matter.

Jack watched Nomad turn to leave and did not call her back. She was almost not there—ethereal, like an echo of someone who had once been. He wondered what it was like being her.

"Jack, she's got to help!" Jenna said from behind him, but Jack shook his head.

"She can't," he said. Nomad was walking away now, and her gait betrayed nothing. *One look*, Jack thought, and he took a deep breath and plummeted into the endless space between potentials, swirling, flitting across the void and closing on one star, always aware of that pulsing, glowing red shape that watched him like the eye of God.

As he reached out to touch what might help him know Nomad, he suddenly realised what the red star was.

Shock struck him from all sides. He gasped and went to his knees, pulled instantly back to stark reality.

"Jack!" Sparky was by his side, clasping him and holding him in a sitting position. Jenna was there too, already looking him over for signs of injury. She checked his eyes, felt his pulse, pressed her hand against his chest. Even Rhali came to him, swaying a little and sighing as she sat and leaned into him.

"It's everything," he said. The words echoed inside his mind.

"What is, mate?" Sparky asked.

"The red star. The . . ." He shook his head, because they did not understand. "Inside. There's something inside I thought was watching me, but it isn't. It just feels like it because it's so alive. So *vital*. It's everything Nomad gave me ready to be passed on. The red star is contagion." He held out his hand and extended his finger, remembering Nomad putting her own finger in his mouth and tasting her on his tongue even now.

She was little more than a silhouette along the street, becoming a shadow.

"I can pass it on," he whispered. Then he fisted his hand. He would not wish this on anyone.

Jenna stared at him for a moment. Then she said, "Come on. She's gone. If she can't help us, we'll help ourselves. We've got to find Breezer again."

"Fifteen hours," Jack said. "That's what we've got."

"Midnight tonight," Sparky said, grim. "At least that gives us something to aim for."

"It's no time at all," Jack said.

Jenna grabbed him beneath the arms and hauled him upright. "Then let's not waste any."

Lucy-Anne ran through the dawn, leaving Hampstead Heath far behind, and with every step she became more convinced that she was being followed.

Others ran with her. She'd become aware of them very quickly, and at first she'd believed that they were chasing her. But she'd hidden away several times to let something pass by, and the monsters showed no signs of pursuing anything. They were animals with human attributes—or humans with animal aspects—and they were heading south into London with motives she could not perceive.

She thought of Jack and the others a lot as she made her own way south. She had no idea how she'd find them, or whether they were even still in the city. Rook had told her that Emily and Jack's mother were safely away at least, but she had no idea what Jack might be doing now. Still, she had to do her best to find them all, and tell them about the bomb.

She passed a small square with a park at the centre. It was overgrown, and the trees' heavy canopies moved with something other than the breeze. Things whispered in there, secret mutterings that might have been about her. She ducked into an open front door and ran through the property, out across the backyard to the alley beyond, over a high wall into another garden, and smashed a window to gain access to another house. Three people were sitting around a table, dried bodies slumped down in their chairs and a meal gone black before them. Lucy-Anne left them to their peace and opened the front door.

The street beyond was silent, and she ran.

Moments later, something emerged from that house and came after her.

She froze in the middle of the street and turned around, but there was nothing to see. *Not one of those monsters*, she thought. She didn't know how she could be so sure, but she clung on to that certainty. It followed, but without malevolence. Perhaps it was an echo of herself, the memory of what she had been or what she might have become had Rook not died. Her dream-shadow.

How she wished she could dream him back again. But she had already seen how that had ended.

"Who are you?" Lucy-Anne shouted. Her loud voice shocked her, echoing between buildings that had been silent for so long. She wondered whether a city could haunt itself. Somewhere so accustomed to the sounds of traffic and human interaction must find silence so strange.

Nothing and no one answered.

"Come out!" she said. "I don't bite." She laughed, perhaps a little manically. She was the only thing she'd met in London that *didn't* bite.

So she moved on instead, glancing back every now and then, seeing nothing, but knowing nonetheless that something saw her.

Along streets, across squares, crossing road junctions clotted with crashed vehicles, Lucy-Anne headed south. She navigated by the sun—it had just risen, so she kept it on her left—and she thought how her father would have chuckled at that. He'd been a Scout leader when he was younger, and though Andrew had always been keen to listen to his dad, Lucy-Anne had been the rebellious one. She could see no sense in camping in the woods with a bunch of kids when she could be causing trouble in town with her friends. There was no point in learning knots and how to build a fire, when finding a pub that would serve them cheap, strong cider was so much more fun. If he could see her now, he'd tell her that she was doing well at gaining her Survival Badge.

She found herself at a T-junction, and across the road was the entrance to an industrial estate. In either direction along the road, the opposite side was lined with the bland grey metal of industrial and business units, and the map on the board at the entrance showed how vast it was. Straight through would be far easier than skirting around it. And at least from what she could see there was less traffic clogging the roads.

As soon as she entered, the noises began. Clanging, dragging. Something following her across rooftops. Something with claws.

She ducked into a large unit and hurried through to the other side. It was stacked with countless boxes of computer screens, millions of pounds in value now worth nothing. They weren't edible, couldn't burn, and would be useless as weapons. She hurried through, still listening for those sounds of pursuit.

She found a fire escape that hung open, the door propped against the sad skeletal remnants of someone who'd wanted to die in the sunlight. She listened, heard nothing.

But she knew that meant little.

Why the hell couldn't I have wandered into a unit that made machine guns and bazookas? she thought as she burst from the door.

Heart hammering, she glanced up at the sky, expecting to see rooks following her progress. But the sky was a bright, blank blue. A beautiful day.

She was thirsty and hungry, her head throbbed, and she was not used to such excessive exercise. But still she ran. She heard something scampering across metal, but she couldn't tell how heavy the something was, nor how far away. She passed by a white van slewed across the road and caught sight of its contents through the open side door—piles of board games, still stacked as if ready for children to take their pick. She thought briefly about jumping into the driver's seat and slamming the door, but if the engine did not fire she might trap herself in there while those pursuing things came for her.

She drew the knife from her belt and held it blade-forward, ready to jab and slash.

Inside another unit, and here the smell was so familiar that it made her gasp aloud. Shoes. Storage racks were stacked with thousands of boxes of new trainers, and a few were scattered around beneath the shelves, bright white and coloured objects that looked so out of place. These were proper running shoes, and she remembered shopping for them with her mother when she had taken up running several years before. She'd watched her mother on a treadmill while the shop assistant analysed videos of her gait, prescribing a certain type of shoe and bringing out her recommendations. Afterwards they had gone to a Starbucks and Lucy-Anne had eaten a shortbread while her mother drank coffee and examined her shoes. The smell conjured this completely detailed memory, and also the more recent dream during which Lucy-Anne had sensed her parents buried in one of London's mass graves.

Tears beaded in her eyes, and she wiped them away.

Approaching a door at the rear of the unit she skidded to a stop. There was a huddle of bodies against the wall, shrivelled, dried skin hanging on grinning skulls. More stories she'd never know. The door was closed, and she checked it quickly for locks. The moment she opened it she wanted to be running, and if she made a noise rattling the handle against locks, then—

Loud impacts sounded from the high metal roof. The noise filled the previously quiet unit. Lucy-Anne cried out in shock, then pressed down the handle and swung the door, darted into the open, and ran.

She crossed a car park and dodged around several cars, then heard thuds behind her as things dropped from the roof.

She stopped and spun around, backing up against a truck sat on flattened tyres. *This is where I make a stand*, she thought, and she was filled with a dreadful sense of foreboding. She had not dreamed this at all. As she saw what faced her, she wished she could have fallen instantly asleep to un-dream it.

She was going to die here, and her bones would be scattered across the moss-covered concrete.

There were three of them stalking closer to her, cautious but confident, and she could sense their hunger. Each breath ended with a gentle growl.

"So what are you supposed to be?" she asked. Her voice wavered, and none of them gave any indication that they had heard.

They were smaller than adult humans, but she had no sense that they were children. Vaguely ape-like, their arms and legs had grown long and thin, yet still wiry and strong. Their naked bodies were covered with a fine brown felt-like fur, and their heads had elongated, mouths protruding and ears flattened against their triangular skulls. The teeth were long and vicious. Their eyes were startlingly human, yet they held little sign of any intelligence she could understand. One of them had a tattoo on its upper arm.

She was certain that they wanted to eat.

"Come on then," she said, waving the knife before her. But she felt no real bravado. She would fight when they came, but she could not kid herself. She might wound one or two of them, but they'd take her down within seconds.

She only hoped it was over quickly.

I'm so sorry, Jack, she thought. *Sparky, Jenna. I'm so sorry. I only hope you get out anyway, but I can't pretend that I'm sad at what's going to happen to London*. She blinked and saw Nomad once more, silhouetted against the nuclear blast that would sweep away all that had gone wrong, and every twisted thing that London had birthed.

When she opened her eyes again, someone else was there.

Lucy-Anne frowned, squinted, trying to make sense of who and what she saw. It was a shadow on the light where no shadow was cast, and when it moved it was like a blind spot in her vision. It flowed from the doorway of the sports shoe unit, and then the ape-things were screeching as it moved amongst them. They darted away, one of them passing so close to her that it collided with the truck's hood, tripped over the bumper and sprawled on the ground, scrabbling for purchase before sprinting away on all fours. One took a huge leap up onto the building's roof and disappeared from view. The others ran across car parks and roads, vanishing between units. In moments they were gone, and Lucy-Anne was alone with whatever, or whomever, had saved her.

Someone new, she thought, but she instantly knew that was wrong. This was someone she *already* knew. She dropped the knife, barely noticing the sound as it struck the ground.

"Rook!" she whispered as the shadow formed before her. A shape where no shape should be, his features manifested from the light, coalescing into the form he used to take. Almost solid, but not quite. Nearly there, but still absent in some fundamental way.

And not Rook.

"My sweet sister," Andrew said.

CHAPTER FOUR
FOURTEEN, THIRTEEN

Hurrying through the streets towards Trafalgar Square once more, Jack felt the weight of responsibility press down on him. He'd seen the way Jenna had been glancing at him, and he knew what she would have to ask again soon: *Why can't you warn everyone?* And he was trying. He truly was. Now that he knew the mystery of that huge red star he was more at peace cruising his internal universe of potential. But that didn't mean he was no longer afraid of it. Perhaps he even feared it more.

He moved from here to there, acknowledging powers he had already tapped, searching for those that might help him now. He discovered amazing things—the ability to implant false memories; cold breath that could freeze; a touch that could turn any solid into a liquid, and then a gas, without heat—but there was nothing to communicate en masse to everyone left in London. The more he looked, the more hopeless it seemed.

Jack wished everything was the way it had been before coming to London.

He thought of Camp Truth, their place in the woods where he, Lucy-Anne, Sparky, Jenna, and sometimes his sister Emily used to gather, collecting scraps of information about London left to them by similarly minded individuals. They'd sit there for long hours, talk, make plans, and then go home to the respective houses to dream away another night. Sparky would work on the old Ford Capri that reminded him so much of his brother, his parents ghosts of what they had once been. Jenna would try to talk to her father, but he was cold now, changed by whatever had been done to him. Lucy-Anne went from home to home, never settling because dreams of her parents and brother would not let her. And Jack would return home to look after his sister Emily. There was help for orphaned families, but there could not be homes for all of them. Doomsday had made too many. So Jack and Emily lived in the home they had shared with their parents, and it was only since leaving that Jack realised that it had really been Emily looking after him.

He could wish for those simpler times, but he did not really want them. Not now he had found his mother and she had escaped London.

And not with what he had now. A curse, perhaps. But some of the things he could do . . .

"I can't," he said, answering no one in particular. But they all seemed to know what he meant. "I'm looking. But there are limits. It's still confusing."

"Maybe we need to be a bit more creative," Sparky said.

"What do you mean?" Rhali asked.

"Dunno. Lateral thinking."

"So let's think laterally while we walk," Jenna said.

Fifteen minutes later they heard motors and ducked into a pub doorway. Jenna tried the handle—locked—and Jack grasped it, eyelids drooping as he delved inside, and he heard the lock's tumblers rolling and clicking. He pulled the handle and the door fell open. They tumbled inside. Sparky shut the door gently, then peered through a dusty window as the engines drew closer.

"You picked the lock with your fingers," Rhali said. "That's pretty amazing."

Jack smiled, blew on his nails, polished them on his jacket.

"Four Land Rovers," Sparky said from the window. They all

ducked down and fell motionless. "Choppers. Couple of them are sitting on the Rovers' roofs. Got rifles. They look . . . odd."

"Odd how?" Jack asked. The vehicles passed by without slowing, and Sparky waited until the engines were fading before answering.

"Like they haven't washed in a while. Dishevelled. You know?"

"Smelly, like you," Jenna said.

"Yeah," Sparky replied. He looked troubled.

"Desperate," Rhali said. Jack realised that she was hunkered down beneath a table, shivering, and he sat beside her. Her eyes were wide and fearful.

"They've gone," he said softly.

"They're hunting," she said. "Looking for revenge. You told us what Reaper and the others did to the Choppers at Camp H. Killed them all."

"Yeah," Jack said. He'd watched the Superior they'd rescued from the cages freezing the Choppers, seen them fall and break apart like fragile statues. No mercy. No humanity.

"So they're looking for us," Jenna said.

"Looking for anyone," Rhali said. She closed her eyes and frowned. "And there are plenty of people around. Lots of movement, through back alleys and beneath the city."

"Movement where?" Sparky asked, still watching from the window.

"Towards where we're going," she said.

Jack stood and went to Sparky. "Clear?"

"Think so. What do you think?"

Jack shrugged. They were all watching him, but it was Jenna who answered.

"Breezer's calling them to him," she said.

"Perhaps. Planning an escape, maybe."

"So he's doing what you can't," Sparky said to Jack. "Communicating with everyone."

"Perhaps," Jenna said. "But he doesn't know how long's left, like we do. We've got to get to him, tell him we should try Miller first. If Breezer just tries an escape, they might all be massacred at the Exclusion Zone."

Jack glanced at his watch. "Come on. Less than fourteen hours."

"That's if what Nomad said was true," Jenna said. "She spooks the hell out of me."

"And me," Jack said. "But I don't think she had a reason to lie."

They left the pub and moved along the street, listening for more engines. Choppers were abroad, intent on murder. Just another day in the toxic city.

It took another hour to reach Trafalgar Square, and from there they moved east until they were close to Heron Tower where Breezer had once made his base. They had to hide twice more from roving Choppers, the second time almost getting caught when a large foot patrol approached along a narrow side street. It was only Rhali's gift that warned them, and they ducked into a Tube entrance with seconds to spare. It was the first time they'd seen a Chopper patrol without vehicles of any kind. There were at least twenty of them, all heavily armed, and it marked another change to their methods.

These soldiers also looked more rag-tag than usual. Jack wondered whether they'd been given their marching orders ahead of the bomb, and had decided to exact revenge on as many Irregulars as they could before leaving London. If so, it was a good sign, because it confirmed that zero hour was still some time away.

Of course, he wouldn't have put it past Miller to not even tell many of his soldiers that the countdown had been triggered.

They hid along the street from the tall office building, listening for danger. Rhali was alert; Jack waited for something to happen.

"Looks deserted," Jenna said.

"That's the way Breezer wants it," Sparky said.

"Yeah, but . . . Rhali said there were loads of survivors coming this way. I thought we'd see some sign of that." Jenna turned to Rhali, who was leaning against Jack. He propped her up. She was growing tired very quickly, her months of abuse at the hands of the Choppers all too apparent.

"The upper floors," Rhali said, nodding. "There are scores of them. And . . . below us. In the tunnels and the Tube lines. I think there's a way into the basement of the building."

"Right," Jack said. "Well. Front door, anyone?"

"We're becoming regular visitors to the place," Jenna said.

"Yeah," Sparky agreed. "They should give us season tickets." His eyes opened wide. "Hope they've got some of those great burgers on the go!"

"The dog burgers?" Jenna asked. "Ewww."

"Dog, cat, rat, don't care what they were. Tasted divine."

As they approached the building, a voice called from shadows. "Howdy, Jack. How's it hanging?" The girl walked from the building's lobby, leaned against the door and put one hand on her hip. She grinned.

"Fleeter," Jack said, surprised.

"Come on in. The kettle's on."

There were so many questions to ask Breezer—about his plans, how he was calling the Irregulars here, why Fleeter was with him, whether he and Reaper were still in contact. But instead Jack opened their conversation with the bombshell.

"We know how long it is until Big Bindy blows."

Breezer seemed shocked to see them. He blinked as if he had dust in his eye, frowned, turned and walked back through the doors, leaving Jack and the others out on the staircase. They'd come up a dozen floors and were breathing hard. Sparky was almost carrying Rhali.

"Still a grumpy bastard," Sparky said.

"Shall we jump off the roof again?" Jenna quipped.

Jack shoved the closing door and marched through. The open plan office area beyond was bustling with two dozen people, and the smell of cooking food wafted through the air. Dividing screens were still ranked a few feet in from the windows, and the people kept to the central area, careful not to cast shadows that might be seen from outside.

"Breezer!" Jack shouted. Heads turned, and a couple of people told him to *Shhhh!* Jack laughed. "It's not a bloody library!" he said. "He hasn't called you all here to sit down quietly to read. You're all going to die!"

"Er, Jack," Jenna said from behind him. Jack raised a hand without looking back. He wasn't sure where the sudden anger had come from, but it felt good to let it flow. Breezer was not the appropriate target—Miller and Reaper were far more suited for that. But right now, he was all there was.

"Jack, don't," Rhali whispered behind him.

"Breezer!" Jack shouted again. The man paused by the dried skeleton of a huge, dead potted plant and turned around. He looked haunted.

"There's nothing we can do," Breezer said. "Clinton died this morning. Remember Clinton?" Jack did. The black man sat in a shopping trolley, snatching truths from the air like flies, affected by the same sickness that was taking root in many of London's survivors. Even Nomad had displayed signs, though she'd denied it.

"It doesn't matter," Jack said. He breathed deeply, trying to make sense of his outburst. Fear contributed, he was sure, and fury at what had happened here, what London had become. Anger, too, at the monster his father had turned into. "We'll get out of London, and out there we'll find a cure."

"It *does* matter," Breezer said. "He was my friend. Every death matters. And at a time like this . . . when so many have died . . . every death matters even more."

Jack felt himself filling up. Tears burned behind his eyes. He nodded, said nothing.

"We've brought as many here as we can," Breezer continued. "Passed the word however we could. Word of mouth, pre-arranged signs. We've even got a woman who can talk with pigeons, use them as messengers. But . . . two groups have already been caught by the Choppers. Three people hanged from Blackfriar's bridge. Two more machine-gunned in Waterloo. I'm doing the best . . ." He gasped, swallowed deeply. "The best I can. And we're going to make a run for it."

"Not yet," Jack said. "Anyone crossing the Exclusion Zone will be slaughtered. Is that the end you want for all these people?" Jack looked around at everyone watching the conversation and wondered what they could all do. It was a room of wonders, but he felt only sadness. He could see several who were obviously in the final throes of the sickness. "Is that what you *all* want?"

No one answered.

"So how long do we have?" Breezer asked.

"Midnight."

"Do you know where it is?"

"Would it matter?" Jack asked.

"Can't you stop it? Nomad's touched you, so can't you disarm it, or take it somewhere else? Or . . . I don't know . . . break it?"

"I don't think so," Jack said. He walked closer to Breezer, lowering his voice in the hope that no one else would hear. His friends most of all. "I'm a mess, Breezer. I have so much inside me, but I'm scared at what I'll do. So no, even if I knew where it was, I don't think I could take that risk. I need time to learn. "

"Don't *have* time," Breezer said.

"No. But we've got a plan. A way to get out, perhaps safely. Are you ready to hear it?"

Breezer seemed to shrink into himself a little, slumping down with the unbearable weight on his shoulders. Perhaps he had burdened himself, but that didn't matter. His tired nod did.

"Anything," he said. "God help us all."

"Not Him," Jack said. "Miller. We need to find him, and you should come with us."

"Let's talk," Breezer said. He looked past Jack and nodded, and at first Jack thought he was greeting Sparky and Jenna again. But when Jack turned around he saw Fleeter standing back by the stairwell doors. She was smiling her usual faint, superior smile.

"Okay," Jack said. "First things first, though. You need to tell me about that."

Nomad lied to me, Lucy-Anne thought. *He's not dead at all!* But her excitement was tempered, and everything here felt like a dream. She was dislocated from her surroundings. Moments before, the creatures had been facing her with bared teeth and curved claws, things that had once been human ready to eat human flesh. Her fear was rich and deep, her senses alert. Now Andrew was before her and everything had changed. Her surroundings had faded into the background. She concentrated on her brother and what he had become.

Not dead at all, but surely no longer alive.

He moved towards her slowly, and she remembered the expression he wore. Four years ago she'd come home from school and Andrew had been waiting for her in the living room, watching TV but obviously distracted. Their parents were at work. Andrew was seventeen then, and he was always home just before Lucy-Anne, ready to get her a snack and make sure she'd had a good day in school, tell her to do her homework, and generally look after her for a couple of hours before their mother arrived home. But from the moment she'd walked through the door that day she'd known that she was in control. Andrew had looked nervous, contrite, and as he'd walked towards her he'd seemed to lessen in stature. *Lucy-Anne, I was playing a game on your iPod and I dropped it in the kitchen, and you know how hard the floor tiles are. I'm sorry. I'll buy you another*. Troubled though their relationship was—he was the Good Boy, the hard worker, the apple in her mother's eye—she could not find it in herself to be angry at him.

He looked the same now as he approached across the cracked concrete car park.

If this is my dream I can change it, she thought, and she glanced towards the industrial unit to her left, willing it to turn to marzipan and icing. But the aluminium sheeting remained, dented and spattered with mould. The windows did not turn into chocolate squares, the drainpipes were not liquorice. *If this is my dream* . . . She closed her eyes and opened them again, but everything was the same.

"You're not here," she said.

"I am," Andrew said. "Enough, at least. But I'm only really an echo. I dreamed myself alive."

"I dream too!" she said.

"You always did. And your dreams drove you to distraction."

Lucy-Anne stepped forward and reached for her brother, but he drifted back as she came closer. His feet barely seemed to move.

"What are you? A ghost? What happened?"

"Ghost is as good a word as any," he said. "And I'll tell you. But you should walk south, and quickly. Those things aren't the only ones moving out of the north today."

"Because of the bomb?"

"Word is spreading," Andrew said.

"Aren't you afraid?"

"Only for you, sister. I'm already dead."

Lucy-Anne closed her eyes and breathed deeply, fighting off a faint. *Only useless women in old movies faint at something like this!* she berated herself. She bit the inside of her lip, pinched the back of her hand, and for a fleeting instant thought that when she looked again he would be gone. That terrified her. So much so that she found herself frozen, unable to move, unwilling to open her eyes in case—

"Lucy-Anne," he said, and she felt something almost stroke her cheek.

Her eyes snapped open and he was there before her, one arm outstretched and his hand moving away. He'd touched her face, just like he used to when she was a little girl and he wanted to show affection. He'd very rarely kissed her. A fingertip to her cheek was his greeting, a gentle touch that said more than any words.

"Oh, Andrew," she said. The tears came at last because she knew he was gone. He echoed to her now, but there was no future for them.

"Quickly," he said, moving backwards, pointing south. "I'll tell you while you walk."

He made her feel safe. She wasn't sure why. He'd seen off the ape-like people, true, but he was hardly there at all. Perhaps it was simply the fact that she no longer felt alone.

"I ran," Andrew said. "After I found Mum and Dad dead in the hotel room I left and ran, as fast as I could, directionless. The streets were filled with bodies back then, so soon after it had happened. And sometimes other people. But most were so scared, so shocked, so alone, that they hid. So I just ran, and I was already dying. Whatever killed everyone else seemed to be acting much slower on me. I didn't know why. I felt myself fading. My strength was filtering away. I fell, and I dreamed myself alive again."

"So you dream, too," Lucy-Anne said, but she should not have been surprised.

"I dreamed of a folly on the hill, and knew what was happening. So I ran on until I found it, and then let everything take its course."

Lucy-Anne reached into her jacket and shirt and brought out the chain and signet ring given to her by Nomad. Andrew's chain, his ring.

"I showed Nomad where to find me," he said.

"You . . ."

"I laid down and died," he said. "Leaning against a wall, still dreaming about *not* dying, because even as I felt myself closing down . . . my heart stopping, my senses fading . . . I was always thinking of you. My poor little sis left all on her own."

"You made yourself a ghost."

"Whatever I am is because of my dreams."

"So, all this time?"

"I've been waiting. But don't be sad for me. It's different for me now."

They left the industrial area behind and moved into residential streets again, countless houses now home only to dried bodies and memories. Lucy-Anne walked with another memory. And even though she knew, the wrench of loss was going to hurt all over again.

"I dream," she said. "And I'm always scared."

"Things change," Andrew said. "Dreams are weird things, the

ones we have even more so. I came to learn that they're like movies that never run the same way twice."

"Movies you can control yourself?" she asked.

"Sometimes you're the director, yes," he said. "But that never lasts."

"I don't understand." She thought of Rook falling into that pit, her dreaming the events again in time to warn him, thinking she'd saved him from that fate. Then he'd fallen again, and the same terrible death had come to claim him.

"I tried so many times when I was your age," he said. "But changing things in your dreams only bleeds over into reality a little, and those bleeds are soon cleared up."

"What are we going to do?" she said, hopelessness washing over her. "What am *I* going to do?"

"Survive," Andrew said. "You're why I'm still here like this. It's *difficult*. And once you're safe, I can stop dreaming at last."

Survive . . . stop dreaming . . . Her brother was a ghost, and Lucy-Anne remembered walking across that strange landscape on London's outskirts, the place where countless bodies had been buried, and knowing that beneath her feet lay her mother and father. The certainty had been shocking, but she'd known it was true because she had already dreamt it. Her life now was starting to feel like one long dream. Her imagination had always taken her to strange places, and sometimes she'd found it teasing her when she could not recall whether a memory was a dream, or vice versa. Many times through her childhood she'd remembered going somewhere with her family that no one else recalled, or believed an event was a dream when her parents and Andrew had very clear memories of it. She'd never thought anything of it. It had felt natural. It was ironic that now she was starting to understand herself and how she dreamed, it felt more alien than ever.

"I'm exhausted," she said. "I can't run forever. I need to . . . I have to . . ." *To dream*, she thought. As she pulled away from Andrew and her surroundings, she could not be certain whether she was falling asleep, or waking up.

People cry out. Flames roar. Someone is wailing as they stagger back and forth across the road, grasping at guts drooping from a terrible wound in their stomach. Their features and hair are burnt away, but Lucy-Anne recognises the clothes.

Nomad is running across the street towards her. She jumps a blazing motorcycle, leaping further than is possible, and barely seems to touch the road as she lands and rushes on. She is the focus of movement in the street, the eye of the storm, and all flames lean away from her.

Lucy-Anne holds up her hands and tries to speak, but her voice has been silenced. *My dream, this is* my *dream, and I can change* everything*!*

But though she knows that she has been here before, she has no control over the scene. She cannot quench the flames, nor can she divert Nomad from her course. Perhaps they have been heading towards this meeting since Doomsday.

Gunfire sounds in the distance, voices, screams, and nearby the pounding of heavy footsteps.

Turn away, she thinks, but Nomad runs onwards. *Step aside*. But the strange woman is determined.

Lucy-Anne opens her mouth, but cannot scream as Nomad runs into her and knocks her to the ground. She tries to punch, but her arm remains by her side, not obeying her dream.

Nomad raises a fist and brings it smashing down on Lucy-Anne's throat.

A burst of light—

The Thames flows sluggishly before her, and to her left she can just see the curve of the London Eye above some buildings. She looks around in a panic for Nomad, knowing that when she sees her the blast will come. There is no stopping it. A sun will grow in London and consume everything, and however much Lucy-Anne wills her dream to change, can she really confront such power?

Nomad killed me, she thinks, feeling the impact on her throat, pressing her hand there, and then she sees her friends. She bursts into tears because they are so solid, so there. They are approaching the river with several other people and they come with purpose. Jack looks older than before, and there's something about him that reminds her of Nomad.

They are much further along the riverbank, and closer to her she sees a group of Choppers squatting down behind concrete benches and a fallen wall. They are watching. And aiming.

We have to go, a voice says. She turns and Andrew is there, walking along the riverbank past a line of long tables covered with the swollen, rotting remains of books. *Lucy-Anne, you don't have long.*

But . . .

She looks at Jack and her friends again, and the other people, and the Choppers slowly standing, ready to fire.

But not now!

Andrew has reached her. He looks more real now than he did back in the reality of London. Perhaps this is how she will best see him from now on—in dreams.

CHAPTER FIVE TWELVE

They talked for half an hour, eating at the same time. Sparky put away three burgers.

While others talked, Jack cruised his mindscape, probing here and there, tasting potentials unknown and powers already dealt, but he could find nothing that might help him locate Miller. If he'd had a drop of the man's blood, or a shred of hair, or an item that had been of sentimental value to Miller, then maybe he could have used one of his fledgling talents to zero in on the man. But he had nothing but a memory of his brutality, evident in the sad form of Rhali. She sat with Jack and shared his warmth, and Jack felt something strong growing between them. Theirs had been a relationship of contact, not words. He found that fundamentally beautiful.

Without any means to find Miller, they could only go to look for him. Breezer would come, and he would bring Guy Morris, the man who could control a person's actions with a whisper. *Order every Chopper to drop their weapons*, he would mutter in Miller's ear. And he would.

"Camp H," Fleeter told them after a while. She sounded confident. "Best place to look if you've no better leads." It was all she contributed to the conversation. Jack went to ask her how she knew, but there was no need. She was Superior, and still enjoyed acting it.

They gave themselves until six p.m. to find Miller and attempt to ensure a safe exit from London. After that, with six hours left until detonation, they would have to rush the Exclusion Zone one way or another. Jack tried to shut out images of thousands of people crossing those bombed, flattened areas and being mown down by machine-gun fire.

He still found Fleeter fascinating. He had seen her killing in cold blood, and yet now she was here, and she seemed different. She looked exhausted, but there was something else about her as well. A brightness, as if she had discovered life again. She'd told Jack about how she'd guided his mother and Emily out of London, and how for a while she'd taken a walk out there, seeing normal people doing normal, everyday things, unaware of the dreadful events just twenty miles from where they lived. This, she'd said, was why she had returned to Breezer and his people. She wanted to help.

She claimed no allegiance with Reaper. But she was still a monster.

Jack would never forget the look in her eyes when she killed, and he could never fully trust her.

From the moment they stepped out into the fresh air once again, Jack knew that something had changed.

"Least we didn't have to jump from the roof this time," Sparky said.

"Pity," Jenna said. "I enjoyed that so much."

"You did, really. Secretly. Deep inside, you want me to carry you upstairs and throw you off."

"You. Carry me up forty flights of stairs. I'd like to see you try."

Sparky grinned and glanced at Jack. "He could."

"I'm not Superman," Jack said. But no one replied to that, and he wondered what everyone really thought of him. He still wasn't sure what he thought of himself. He feared the potential he carried inside, and worried that they were untried, untested, and liable to backfire if he used them all too rashly. But perhaps it was merely a question of confidence. Maybe he needed to grow used to bearing such power.

Time would tell. And as he breathed in the strange London air and sensed the changes occurring, he knew that he would be testing more powers very soon.

"Something's different," he said.

"Spidey senses tingling," Sparky said.

"What is it, Jack?" Rhali asked. She touched his arm, held his hand. She'd not eaten much—said she was not used to such food, and that in captivity they had sometimes forgotten to feed her for days. But she already seemed stronger.

"Can't you feel it?" he asked them all. Sparky and Jenna walked together, Rhali was with him. Fleeter strolled slightly ahead of them, automatically taking the lead. Breezer and Guy Morris accompanied them, quiet and tense. They never liked travelling in the open like this.

"No," Breezer said as if stating the obvious.

Jack was not aware that he was using any particular power. Between blinks he searched inside, but he'd touched no star, and there was no taste of Nomad on his tongue. Perhaps using what she had given him was becoming second nature. But that made him wonder just what he was turning into.

"Rhali," he said. "You sensed it."

"I still sense movement to the north," she said. "And moving closer."

"But whatever's coming towards us is different," he said. "Not . . . human."

"Oh, dandy," Jenna said.

Jack looked around at the high buildings, absorbed the silence. "The whole city's holding its breath."

"We need to move," Breezer said, eyes wide. "And quickly."

"What is it?" Jack asked.

"The north. That's where the monsters went after Doomsday. Not many people go up there, and some who do don't come back."

"Monsters?" Jenna asked.

"Evolve caused physical changes in some people," Breezer said. He nodded at Fleeter. "You know."

"I only know the stories," she said. "Wolf men. Bird people. Flesh eaters."

"Oh, super," Sparky said.

"And now they're moving into the city," Rhali said.

"Oh, even *more* super."

Rhali breathed deeply, clasping Jack's hand tighter for support. "There's a small group a mile away," she said. "Moving . . . too quickly."

"Right," Jack said. "The river. A boat. Let's go. Fleeter?"

Did she looked a little afraid? He wasn't sure. Such a look might have been another version of her smug smile, or a trick of the light. But just before she flipped out with a *smack!* and went to check their route, she locked eyes with Jack, and he saw something dark staring back.

They headed for the river. Jack wondered why no one had mentioned the north before, and the people and things who lived there. But he supposed there had been no need. London was a vastly changed place, and it could be that the north had become as remote as the outside world. When he had a chance, he would ask Fleeter about it.

They moved as silently and quickly as possible. He saw things that days ago would have traumatised him for life, but which now were merely another part of the landscape. Two withered, dried shapes hung side by side from nooses suspended from second storey windows. A pram sat in the middle of the road, a mess of blankets and clothing inside, mother dead on the road with her skeletal fingers curled around one wheel. A bus had driven into a DVD store, and the silhouettes of its dead passengers were just visible through the dusty windows.

"No one buried them all," Rhali said. Jack was surprised, and then he remembered that the Choppers had caught her soon after Doomsday. She'd been shut away since then.

"There was no one left to do it," he said. "London is their mausoleum."

A *clap!* and Fleeter reappeared beside the bus. She projected her usual aloof smile, but swayed where she stood, reaching out to the bus for balance. She closed her eyes for a moment, breathing deeply.

"We're clear from here to the river," she said. "No Choppers. But what's coming from that way *isn't* safe." She nodded back the way they'd come.

Both Sparky and Jenna looked at Jack expectantly. He in turn looked at Breezer and raised his eyebrows.

"You know what Guy can do," Breezer said. Jack nodded. He'd seen the small, thin man in Camp H telling the Choppers to drop their weapons. "Whether his powers of suggestion will work on whatever's coming down from the north . . ." He shrugged. Beside him Guy remained silent, offering nothing.

"Guess it's all on you, then," Jenna said to Jack.

"I don't want to kill anyone else," he said.

"You might not have—" Fleeter began, but Jack cut her off.

"I'm not like you! Come on!"

They moved less cautiously than they would have normally, trusting Fleeter's observations, and soon they were closing on the river. Breezer said he and the Irregulars kept two boats moored there, engines services and fuel tanks full, just in case they were ever needed. But they hadn't started the motors in over a year. Too noisy, too risky.

Close to the river was an open square, landscaped and with several large stone sculptures on marble plinths. The sort of place office workers might have come to for lunch, and tourists might have chosen to have their pictures taken with the river and London skyline in the background. An ice cream van sat in one corner on flattened tyres, a line of bodies sprawled on the ground before its open window. It illustrated again the speed with which disaster had befallen London. In the distance, on the other side of the river, Jack could just make out the upper third of the London Eye, its graceful arc marred by the damage from the helicopter crash that had started everything.

"They're coming," Rhali said, and moments later four shapes burst from a side street across the road from the square.

"What the hell are *they*?" Sparky said. No one answered. Everyone drew close together and squatted down, sheltering behind a sculpture but knowing that it would not protect them for long.

Jack probed inward and prepared himself, balancing two talents, ready to use either. His heart hammered and he felt sick. Even though these things no longer looked quite like people, the thought of killing them was horrible.

A woman wore flowing clothes, but they did nothing to camouflage her lengthened limbs, or her scaled skin. Her eyes shone with a purple membrane, and her teeth were long and crowded into her mouth. She hissed as she ran by, tongue tasting them on the air. A man followed, bounding on hands and feet. He was naked, body elongated. Long spines protruded from his back, and on either side grew rudimentary wings. Blood dripped down his side, and when he roared it sounded full of pain. He followed the woman, away from them and towards the river. But the other two arrivals slowed as they crossed the square. The two women hooted to each other as they both turned to stare at the huddled group.

"Don't think much of yours, mate," Sparky whispered, and Jack almost guffawed with nervous laughter. But he had to be in control. Everyone here was depending on him.

The women's skin was so pale it was almost translucent, bodies incredibly thin, breasts reduced to nothing. There was something fluid about them, both in the way they moved and how they looked—as if their skins contained molten innards, rather than flesh and blood. They hooted again, and countless tiny tentacles extruded from their forearms and palms, waving as if caught in a breeze.

"Do you think—?" Jenna began, and then both women roared and came at her. Their inhuman voices cried hunger.

Jack stood and pointed at them, keeping his arms and shoulders relaxed, and as he exhaled both women were lifted from the ground. He held them there using the talent he'd first seen in Puppeteer, and he felt the potential thrumming through his arms—he could throw, squeeze, *crush* them. They thrashed and squirmed, and one grasped hold of the sculpture. Her tentacles flexed and curled around the concrete, pulling hard, but Jack only felt the slightest tension. His power was not muscular.

"What now?" Rhali asked.

"Ice cream van," Jack said. "Doors."

Sparky, Jenna and Breezer rushed to the van and tugged open the driver's door. Jenna winced back at whatever was inside, but Sparky turned and gestured to Jack.

Jack started walking, still pointing, and the two strange women drifted through the air before him.

"Stand back," he said, and he guided them in through the door.

Breezer slammed it shut.

"Stay in the van," Guy said, and Jack felt an intimate, sickening sensation inside his head. *If I was in the van, I'd stay inside*, he thought.

He knew at that moment that he could bear that talent as well, given time. Its star was open to him.

But as well as their bodies, these women's minds were sufficiently altered from human to apparently make them immune to the man's words. They kicked and banged at the door as Sparky shoved it closed. Thin tentacles squirmed through the lock and around the door's edge, and Jack had only moments to reach out with his mind and snap the locks closed. He did the same for the other door, and also the wide hatch that led from the cabin back into the ice cream van's rear area. He didn't think it would hold the women for long. He caught a brief glimpse of one of their inhuman faces at the window, and he thought perhaps they wanted to feed.

It did not bear thinking about, and they all ran as one from that place of sculptures and danger, sprinting across the wide paved walkway and towards the Thames.

"Which way?" Jenna asked Breezer. He pointed left. There was an iron fence lining the river, but five hundred feet away Jack could see a break in the fence and a walkway leading across to several pontoons. Two of them sat unevenly in the water, the large boat moored to one resting on a slant on the river's bed. But another pontoon floated upright, and he thought he could see the two boats Breezer had mentioned.

From behind them they heard glass smashing. The trapped things would be out in moments. Jack was not afraid of being caught by them, because he would not let that happen.

He was afraid of killing them.

"Jack!" someone shouted. He looked around, wondering who they'd left behind, but they were all there. As he caught Sparky's eyes, his friend's mouth fell open in shock.

"Jack!" the voice called again, and then he recognised it. Lucy-Anne.

She was along the path from them, running and waving frantically. There was someone with her . . . or was there?

"Lucy-Anne!" he shouted. He forgot the danger they were in, the people he had killed, the weight of danger crushing them from all angles. For that brief instant all was delight, and he wanted to greet his dear friend with a hug. He waved at her to come with them, and heard Jenna's and Sparky's delighted laughter.

And then Lucy-Anne shouted again. "*Get down!*"

Between them, several Choppers stood from behind a fallen wall and three heavy benches. Without warning, the shooting began.

Lucy-Anne shouted one more time, and then a Chopper turned and started shooting at her and she fell and rolled, pressing herself flat against a kerb, the gutter barely deep enough to protect her. Bullets impacted the sidewalk about her and plucked at her clothing, her hair, and kissed the back of one leg with icy pain that quickly turned lava-hot. *Oh no oh no!* she thought, again and again, because she had not dreamed the end of this. Whatever fate had in store for her and her friends today had yet to be played out.

"Andrew!" she yelled, but his wraith was no longer with her. "Jack!" she called instead.

More gunfire, shouting, and behind the impacts she heard running feet. She glanced up and around, terrified that at any moment a bullet would find her head. At least she wouldn't know. She could not comprehend the instant change from alive to dead an impact on her brain would cause, but right then it did not frighten her. What scared her was not being here anymore to tell her friends about the bomb. They were all she had left, and with every atom of her body she did not want to let them down.

Someone screamed, androgynous in their agony.

"Drop your—" a voice shouted, and gunfire erupted from a different direction. *More of them!* she thought. She risked a glance above the shallow kerb.

A Chopper was running towards her, barely thirty feet away, rifle held across his chest. As he saw her he paused and shouldered his rifle, and then he was smashed forwards in a haze of blood, pavement beneath him fracturing, a roar accompanying his death. Blood spattered the ground close to Lucy-Anne and she rolled back, stood, not knowing which way to turn.

Beyond the dead Chopper were three others, all of them dead and leaking across the ground. And beyond them, Jack and his friends were dragging a shape across the pavement, huddled low and heading for the cover of a boat ride ticket kiosk. Lucy-Anne couldn't see who had been hit. She started running.

More gunfire burst from a building to her right, flashing from two second floor windows. The kiosk blurred, and splinters and shards of wood flicked at the air. They wouldn't last a second behind there. Barely aware of what she was doing—not knowing what she *could* do—Lucy-Anne changed direction and ran for the building. It was a grand old structure, perhaps an up-market office block, and the storeys were tall. So the two Choppers fell at least fifteen feet when they were thrown from the windows.

Lucy-Anne winced at the crunch of breaking bones, but the silence that followed was a blessing.

A shape appeared in one window—a stocky woman in a short skirt, holding onto the window frame and looking down at what she had done. There was another, taller shape behind her, but Lucy-Anne could not make it out. Not quite. But she had seen that silhouette before, and she thought perhaps it was Reaper.

One of the Choppers was still alive, crawling away from the

building in a vain attempt to escape. Lucy-Anne ignored them. They were a person in pain, but so was she. And they might have just killed one of her friends.

She ran. Focussed on the kiosk, ignoring the dead Choppers she passed and their spreading blood and broken weapons, she started sobbing uncontrollably as she saw Jack stand and look her way. And he smiled and opened his arms as she drew close, pulling her into a warm, loving, living embrace that made her, for the first time since Rook, glad to be alive.

There was nothing Jack could do. Guy Morris had been killed by a bullet in the throat as he'd tried yelling at the Choppers to drop their weapons. Two inches to the left or right and perhaps Jack could have healed the wound and saved him. But his spine had been smashed and he'd quickly bled out.

He embraced Lucy-Anne, so pleased to see her, to feel her warmth. Sparky and Jenna came and hugged them both, and for a brief, beautiful moment Jack wasn't sure who was crying and who was not. When Fleeter reappeared with a clap and they parted, he realised that some of the tears were his.

Not relinquishing contact with Lucy-Anne, he turned to Fleeter. She still smiled, but looked more exhausted than ever.

"So where is he?" Jack asked.

"Gone."

"He's watching over us."

Fleeter shrugged. "He cares. About what you're doing."

"Yeah. Right." Jack was both furious and relieved. He'd been gathering his own strength, about to unleash his own shout again, when his father had killed the Choppers. More blood spilled to stain the London streets, and Jack's memory, forever. But at least this time it had not been at his hand.

"So where is he now?" Sparky asked.

Fleeter glanced at Sparky, then back at Jack and Lucy-Anne. "Looks like you found your girlfriend."

Jack could have punched her. He saw the mischief in her eyes as she looked over Jack's shoulder at Rhali standing behind him, and he couldn't believe she was doing this now, with the smell of death rich in the air. It was as if murder enlivened her.

"We really need to go!" Breezer said. He trotted along the riverbank path, skirting around the dead Choppers. From back the way they'd come, Jack heard more smashing glass, and a high, loud hooting sound that made his balls tingle with fear.

They ran. Lucy-Anne and Jenna went together, talking, their laughter perhaps a little too high and mad. Jack grasped Rhali's hand and squeezed, and when she squeezed back he felt a rush of gratitude. He hoped she felt the warmth developing between the two of them—if not, he would make sure he told her what he felt at the first opportune moment. But she also recognised the strength of friendship and history between him and Lucy-Anne. He hadn't even scratched the surface of how incarceration had affected her, but it seemed her mind was still sharp.

Still running, Jack leaned across to kiss her cheek, and she surprised him at the last moment by turning to him. Their lips met, and for a blissful instant nothing else mattered.

"Well, now," Rhali said as they mounted the ramp leading down to the pontoon.

"Yeah," Jack said. They had to let go hands and walk in single file, but he thought their touch would last forever.

CHAPTER SIX ELEVEN

"Andrew's with me," Lucy-Anne said. "He knows. He . . ." She trailed off, confused and scared.

"I didn't see Andrew," Jack said. *But* did *I see someone with her? Just for a moment?*

"He came with me. From Hampstead Heath. Rook and I went there to find him, and Nomad was there, and Rook fell and I ran, but then Andrew came to me and he's . . . dead, but not gone. Not quite gone. He brought me down here . . . and I dreamed I'd meet you all here!" She went from confused to delighted, her expression changing in a flash as she looked from Jack to Sparky to Jenna. Then her smiled dropped again as if punched from her face. "There's a bomb!"

"We know," Jenna said. She held Lucy-Anne and it was strange to see. The girl they all knew was not someone to be held or pitied. "The Choppers planted it, Miller triggered it. We've got maybe eleven hours."

"You know?" Lucy-Anne asked. "Why? Who's Miller? How did you find out?"

"There's so much to tell you," Jack said. "And it sounds like you have a lot to tell us. But your leg's bleeding. Here. Let me—"

Lucy-Anne frowned and pulled away from Jenna, and for a moment it looked like she was going to jump back onto the pontoon before they'd even set off.

"Andrew?" she said, scanning the shore. "Andrew."

"You're back with us now," Jack said.

"Jack's told me a little about you," Rhali said kindly.

Lucy-Anne's face crumpled. The tears came without warning, and after a few deep sobs she rubbed them away just as quickly. "Oh Jack, I'm so tired," she said. When she slumped down, Sparky was already there to catch her. She rested her head on his shoulder and closed her eyes.

"Breezer?" Jack asked.

"Yeah." He pushed a button and the boat's engine coughed and grumbled, but did not catch.

From somewhere out of sight on shore they heard the hooting from those strange, wild women.

"Breezer, now would be a good time for us to escape."

"Yeah." He pushed the button again, keeping it pushed in so that the engine turned and grumbled and turned again, and then it caught. Clouds of smoke belched from twin exhausts at the vessel's rear, and Breezer slumped in relief.

"Your London river tour is about to begin," he said, pushing the throttle forward. The boat bumped against the pontoon and then moved away.

Those women had something of the water about them, Jack thought. But when he saw them appear along the riverbank at the metal railing, they paused and watched the boat chugging away downriver. He sensed a moment of indecision in them as they seemed ready to give pursuit. But then they leapt into the water and swam in the opposite direction, moving incredibly quickly across the water's slugging surface before diving and disappearing from view.

"Trick?" Jenna asked. Jack wasn't sure. He readied himself, prepared to fight them if he had to. He imagined their slick fingers and tentacles curling around the boat's safety rail, their unnatural faces peering at him, showing him their teeth. But a few moments later he saw them surface and scramble up onto the opposite bank, and they disappeared south of the river without another backward glance.

"Weird," Jenna said.

"Yeah. Maybe there're easier pickings that way."

No one replied. None of them wanted to discuss what, or who, those easier pickings might be.

The boat was a small tourist vessel that promised "The most picturesque views of London, bar none." How one boat could offer any more picturesque views than any other, Jack did not know. But right then he thanked the owners of the *City Sleeker* for running their business on the Thames. He hoped they'd not been in London when Evolve hit, but disaster had struck at the height of summer, and he knew it unlikely. He didn't want to ask Breezer about where they'd found the *Sleeker*, nor how many bodies it had contained.

It was about thirty feet long, the front half open, the stern covered with a glass canopy. The cabin was right at the stern, raised a little from the canopy so that the captain could see along the length of the boat. Seating was arranged looking outward, not ahead, with an open area of deck down the centre for those who wished to stand. Life belts were strung beneath seats, and on the covered area's roof was a lifeboat, strapped down and covered in a tarpaulin. No one wished to be reminded of their vulnerability.

Jack and Sparky uncovered the lifeboat and familiarised themselves with its release mechanism. None of them wanted to go into these waters, and with the amount of detritus in the river, the chance of hitting a submerged object was too high for comfort.

Breezer piloted them upstream. The others sat within the glass-enclosed area, still feeling exposed. The engine sounded incredibly loud.

Lucy-Anne was not asleep, but she seemed to be staring into space. Jack held her leg and gently eased her bleeding. The bullet had barely grazed her, but she would still bruise. Then she went back to her silent contemplation. He guessed she had a lot to think through, and when they were safer he'd talk to her.

Safer. It was not a word that meant much right then.

Rhali watched the river banks, casting out her senses, discovering several groups of people moving around the city to the north. There were some to the south as well, and she quickly gathered a picture of movements which she communicated to the others.

"I think some of them are Choppers," she said. "And some of them are just . . . normal people. Like you." She nodded at Breezer.

"Irregulars," Jenna said.

"Whatever name they wish to use," Rhali said dismissively. "But some of them—a lot of them—are strange. Changed. Like those women we saw. And they're tortured."

Jack glanced at Rhali.

"Not like me," she said. "I mean they're in pain from what they have become. Imagine changing so much. Imagine what such physical changes must feel like?"

"They're going the wrong way to be fleeing the city, even if they know about the bomb," Jack said. "They're coming south for something else."

"They *do* know," Lucy-Anne said. "And Nomad told me they're not so monstrous. I think she meant that they know exactly what they're doing. They're intelligent."

"Great," Jack said.

"Yeah," Sparky said. "Long as what they're doing doesn't involve eating us."

Lucy-Anne started crying, grasping her friend, burying her face in his jacket. Jack had never seen her so vulnerable. Whatever had happened to her, whatever she had seen, must have been terrible. He wondered what had happened to the boy Rook.

But he feared that finding out would only add to the weight of responsibility he felt. He had no power to counter that, no unknown star in his new universe that could temper the fates being piled on him. Rhali, the poor girl who'd had terrible things done to her, and he'd not even had the time to ask what. Lucy-Anne, his old girlfriend, confused and suffering and with so much to tell. Sparky and Jenna, still with him because they valued their friendship so much. Breezer. Even his father. That bastard Reaper, following him and protecting him, or perhaps merely playing with him now that Miller was no longer such an exciting plaything.

The bomb, London, Nomad, his expanding starscape of wonders, and his potential for contagion.

He wished he could shrug them all off and be on his own, unhindered and free. He closed his eyes but it didn't work. He hadn't chosen all this at all; it had been thrust upon him. Nomad was to blame.

When he opened his eyes Jenna was staring at him, and he thought of reaching out and touching her, as Nomad had touched him. His vision swam red. Red, for danger. *What would I give her?* he thought, and then his musings were interrupted.

"Where it all began," Sparky said. He had moved into the boat's open bow and was staring to starboard, and they all watched as the London Eye came into view around a bend in the river. It was still quite awesome, even with everything it represented. The scar in its upper reaches was charred black and angry, and somewhere behind it on the embankment lay the remains of Nomad's helicopter. She had been Angelina Walker back then, a normal human being. She had changed everything.

"Maybe twenty minutes from here," Breezer said from the cabin. "Make the most of the rest."

The strange new smells of London, the sights, and occasionally the sounds—today this truly was the best view anyone could have of London, from the river at least. The Houses of Parliament remained as impressive and imposing as ever. Next to them, the clock on Big Ben's tower was frozen at a moment in time, the bell now silent. The moment meant nothing but the end of the clock's constant round of maintenance.

The quiet and stillness along the river was as unnatural as in the rest of the city, because this was a place built for life, bustle, and commerce. The only movements were the bow wave from their boat blurring the water's surface, and the flights of birds startled aloft by the engine. Sunlight reflected from dusty windows, hiding grotesque truths inside. Uneven huddles of clothing along the north and south embankments were too distant to make out fully, and for that Jack was glad. He knew they were bodies, but not seeing them meant he could pretend they were something else.

The stillness could not last forever. Jack saw the first movements just as they passed beneath Waterloo Bridge, and for an instant he was afraid they were Choppers. They'd be drawn to the noise for sure, but he'd hoped their journey would be so rapid that they'd be out of the boat and gone before anyone arrived. It could be that Reaper was still shadowing them—Fleeter didn't seem concerned with sharing that information, and Jack was not going to humour her by asking—but Jack would still ready himself to protect them. Reaper played games.

"See them?" Rhali asked.

"How long have they been there?" Jack asked.

"I first sensed them just a few minutes ago. They're not following us, I don't think. They're just coming to cross the river."

"Like those weird women."

"Yes."

"So what is it they suddenly want south of the river?" Sparky asked.

Jack glanced at Lucy-Anne, but she seemed not to be listening. Eyes open, she was somewhere else.

"Maybe they know the bomb's in the north and they're running from it," Jenna suggested.

"Maybe," Jack said. He was watching the movement on the north bank, trying to make out who or what they were. Everyone left alive in London had been touched by Evolve, but now he had discovered a new dimension to Doomsday's curse—physical change. Nomad might have said they weren't monstrous, but neither were they natural.

He sensed Sparky and Jenna watching him, and knew exactly what they wanted. He sighed. A brief burst of anger set his limbs tingling, and he rounded on his friends ready to confront them. *I can't magic our way out of everything!* he wanted to shout. *Not with everything else! Why don't one of you do something?* And he could have reached out and touched them, given them the chance.

But Rhali was looking at him as well, and everything she had been through seemed to reflect London's fate. Misused, tortured, abused, she was not what she should have been. His heart sank and he felt an intense sickness at the unfairness of things. *She's so pretty and bright, she shouldn't be anything but beautiful.*

"I'm never going to let anything bad happen to you again," he said to the girl. Her eyes glimmered with tears, and he looked at everyone else in the boat. He was surprised, and humbled, to see that they already felt included in what he'd said.

He tasted Nomad on his tongue, and he heard her voice telling Lucy-Anne that they were not so monstrous. But he was not at all certain of that.

Rhali's gift came to him quickly. Holding her hand, he easily homed in on her point of light and plunged in, her talent blooming in him like an ever-expanding sun. It was both terrifying and beautiful, and he realised that he revelled in this. His new universe scared him, but he would have been inhuman if it did not. Yet he also found it wonderful.

He cast his senses up and out and felt the movement of groups of people close to where they were, projected onto his perception as warm glows on a sea of ice. Those nearby were clear, while further away they became smaller and more remote. But it was the closer movements that interested him.

Jack took hold of what he felt and travelled once again. He quickly focussed on one mass movement. There were perhaps eight of them, travelling in a loose group along the path of the river towards a bridge. He homed in on one, attaching himself to its heat and light and life.

He found the star he sought and plunged towards it. As he did so, it became the mind of another.

Jack had planned questions, sought answers, but both became abstract. This was like nothing he knew or understood, and for what felt like forever he tumbled and swirled in this alien place, trying to grab and hold onto something, *anything*, that made sense. It was only when he accepted that there was little sense to be made that his fall became more controlled.

This was such an alien mind that he might as well have tried conversing with a tree, or a river. But there were still images here that he could perceive, and with some concentration, understand.

He knew what it sought.

"Jack? Jack!"

Slap!

Reality rushed in, a sickening sensation that was nothing like the gentle flow of waking up. Everything hit home, and when he quickly sat up sickness flooded his mouth. He leant sideways and spat it out, breathing shallowly, willing himself not to puke up everything else.

"Gross," Sparky said.

"You slap me hard enough?" Jack asked.

"Hey, gotta take the opportunities given to me. You're lucky I don't carry a hammer."

"Thanks, mate."

"Yeah. Well." Sparky's voice barely hid his concern, and Jack looked up, making an effort to smile. It was difficult.

"What did you see?" Rhali asked. She was sitting on a bench, looking weak and drained. He wondered whether he had taken anything from her.

"They . . ." Jack paused, knowing that they were all listening, but unable for a moment to continue. "They'll still human, deep inside, though barely. Still have their loves and lives, hopes and fears. And yet . . . so different. Changed so much. And it hurts them."

"Good!" Lucy-Anne said. Her blank expression did not change, though her voice was filled with venom.

"They can't help what they've become," Jack said. "And they're doing their best. To survive. To find the bomb, and stop it."

"They know where it is?" Sparky asked.

Jack nodded. "South of here, across the river. I saw their destination, and I think I recognised it. Visited it with school a few years back. Imperial War Museum."

"So they're all going there to stop it," Jenna said.

"To try." Jack nodded and stood up, looking across the silent, dying city. "They barely have a concept of outside. London is their only home now, and they're doing their best to save it."

"Can they?" Jenna asked. "I mean, those women we saw didn't seem, I dunno . . . intelligent."

"I saw gargoyle people," Lucy-Anne said. "Trying to fly. They had claws. And a woman like a dog, pissing against a tree. A man like a monkey. And the worm." She looked up, but her expression did not change. "There was the worm that ate Rook."

"So he is gone," Jack said softly.

"I dreamed him well again, but it still took him in the end. I dream the future. Change it. And it only changes back again." She frowned and ran her hand through her short hair. "I think that's what happens, at least."

"Did they kill your brother too?" Sparky asked gently. His own brother was dead in London, and Lucy-Anne would know that. Such loss was something else that had forged their friendship.

"Oh no, Andrew's still . . . he's still around." She glanced around the boat as if expecting him to appear. "He said he dreamed himself alive, so when he *did* die, he didn't quite go."

"He's a ghost?" Jenna asked.

"I guess." Lucy-Anne fingered a chain around her neck, looking out across the river.

Jack had seen so much that he had little trouble believing in ghosts. But right now, wherever or whatever Andrew was did not matter.

"Knowing where it is doesn't help us much," he said. He looked at Fleeter sitting at the bow of the boat. She had been taking all this in without comment, smiling her annoying smile. "You're sure Miller's still at Camp H?"

"No," she said. "It was just an idea."

Jack felt anger rising, but he drove it down. He needed calmness now more than ever.

"Fifteen minutes," Breezer said. "We'll know soon enough, one way or another."

CHAPTER SEVEN TEN

The bodies were still there. The ruin of Camp H seemed untouched since the brief, terrible battle of the day before, and the scene had a familiarity that made Jack's skin crawl. The metal containers in which Miller and the Choppers had made their base—a prison and vivisection centre for the Irregulars and Superiors they managed to capture—were crushed by the forces unleashed upon them. Several dead soldiers lay alongside one container, and scattered across the clearing in the container park were fifteen or twenty more corpses. It was difficult to tell exactly how many—Jack had seen them frozen by the Superior he'd helped rescue, then shattered into pieces by his father's deadly whisper. Those pieces had now thawed. Carrion birds were feeding on them, and he could see the red streaks across the concrete where some had been dragged away during the night.

Miller sat in his wheelchair beside the ruined prison container. He was alone, and at first glance Jack couldn't tell whether he was alive. But he reached out with his mind and touched upon the chaos of Miller's thoughts, and as they emerged from between containers, the madman's eyes were upon them. He'd gathered dead soldiers' jackets across his lap, around his shoulders and over his head. He was huddled down in his chair. Jack could only see a small pale spread of skin, and the glimmer of one eye. He might have been the Emperor from *Star Wars*, but if so he ruled a doomed empire.

"Stay on your toes," Jack said. "Rhali?"

"I think we're alone now," she said.

"Could be a song there, somewhere," Sparky quipped.

Jack led the way. Breezer came with him, and behind them were Sparky, Jenna and Rhali.

Fleeter had flipped out as soon as they'd moored and left the boat, saying that she was going to scout the way ahead. Jack hadn't even bothered trying to call her back. She had her own agenda.

"That's far enough!" Miller called. There was something wrong with his voice; a growl, rough-edged.

Jack laughed. "What, Miller? Have you got us covered?"

"Monsters," Miller muttered. His words echoed from the container piles around Camp H.

"Yeah, right," Rhali said. "*We're* the monsters." Her voice was quiet. But there was fear and fury there, and Jack had never heard her so alive.

"I said that's far enough!"

Jack and his companions stopped.

"Why?" Jack asked.

"I don't want to be seen," Miller said.

"What did he do to you this time?"

"Your father, you mean?"

"Reaper," Jack said. "He's no longer my father."

"Oh, he is, boy. And you've got it in you too. I can see it in your eyes, the way you stand. You're dripping with power, and when you use it, you'll become a monster as well."

Jack tried to blink away the memory of those three Choppers he'd killed. He was afraid Miller might see it.

"Why aren't you dead?" Rhali spat.

"I am!" Miller laughed. It was a horrible, high giggle, made more dreadful because his body and wrapped clothing barely moved at all.

"We don't have time to piss around, here," Jack said quietly. He started walking forward again, trying not to see the human parts scattered around his feet, and trying not to remember the terrible things he had seen inside those containers. In the larger collection of containers, the research rooms where the unfortunates had been dissected and stored. And in the smaller unit, the prison where they'd kept those due for experimentation. Monstrous. Almost unthinkable. And the man responsible for all of it was this wretched thing before him.

Jack's anger rose again. He'd already held a gun to this bastard's head and refrained from pulling the trigger. But he had greater weapons than guns.

Far greater.

"Stay back!" Miller said. A hand emerged from the clothing, palm out. Two fingers were missing, their stumps ragged and wet.

Jack stopped. "I can help you." The idea of fixing some of Miller's wounds was reprehensible. Yet even thinking that way gave Jack a sense of inner peace. *I'm better than him*, he thought. But there was nothing superior about that idea. It was a fact, and even entertaining the idea that he could help Miller was proof of that.

"Help?" Miller said, and then he laughed again. He slumped in his chair as he did so, as if each time he exhaled he shrank a little more.

"I can't help him," Rhali said. Jack wasn't aware that she'd advanced with him, but he would not tell her to wait. She'd been through too much for that. There was no violence in her, but she still had rage to expend somewhere, somehow.

When they drew close to Miller, and he threw back the jackets and hoods covering him, everything seemed to change.

There was barely a human left. Reaper must have worked on Miller for some time after Jack and his friends and family had left, and perhaps some of his Superiors had taken a turn as well. The woman who could freeze flesh with a breath. The knife man. Perhaps someone who could pin life to something that should be dead.

He wore a white surgical mask across his face, but it could not hide the mutilation. His ears had been torn off. One eye was missing, and both eyelids had been sliced away, leaving his remaining eye wide and white and frantic, and flowing with moisture. His nose was broken and caked with dried blood, and beneath the mask his jaw seemed to protrude too far to the left. It moved constantly, as if he were chewing cud.

"Oh, my God," Rhali whispered.

Miller chuckled. "Like what you see?" He moved more clothing aside.

Reaper had taken more from each of his legs, removing the left all the way up to the groin. His left arm was twisted and broken, thumb and three fingers removed so that only the middle finger remained. Perhaps Reaper had thought it an amusing gesture, though Jack doubted he had any humour left in him at all. Miller's shoulders were bruised and lacerated. There was nothing visible that was untouched, and no telling what horrors the bloodied, fouled clothing still hid. He stank. It was pitiful and sickening, but Jack looked deep for any shred of sympathy.

"No," Rhali said. "No, I don't like it. But you deserve it. Every cut and stab and gouge you've made on another innocent has been visited upon you. I could never hurt you, Miller, much as I want to. I kept my humanity, even through everything you did to me. The starvation, the deprivation. The *humiliation*. So I could never avenge myself on you. But I see you now . . ." She went close to him, too close for Jack's comfort, but Miller merely winced back into his chair. "And I hope it hurts." Then Rhali turned her back on Miller forever and glanced sadly at Jack as she walked away.

"Okay," Jack said. He nodded at the ruined shell of the vivisection suite. "I think in there would be an appropriate place to talk."

"You're going to torture me?" Miller drawled, totally unconcerned.

"No," Jack said. "No, probably not."

There were still bodies inside. They might have died when Jack and Fleeter first pushed them over—when flipped, gentle movements would translate as incredibly fast, violent actions in the real world. But he thought it likely the Superiors had returned to finish the job. Jack averted his eyes, but the stench of rot was cloying.

He wheeled Miller into the vivisection room. The metal table was stained with dried blood, and more blood was puddled where buckets had been kicked away from the drainage points. Walls were deformed, the ceiling crushed down, tools of torture scattered across the floor. Jack thought perhaps Miller had spent some time on this table at Reaper's hand.

Breezer came with him and stood with arms folded across his chest. He could not hide his disgust at the man in the wheelchair, and it was not only at his appearance. Jack had not asked Breezer how many Irregulars he'd known who had been taken by the Choppers, but it was a fair bet that parts of some of them resided in sample jars in the next room.

"So all this torture and pain and death, and what did you find out?" Breezer asked. "Was it worth it? Has any of this been worth anything?"

"I'm too tired to talk about it," Miller said. "We're so close to the end that none of it matters anymore. Big Bindy will blow in . . ." He turned his mutilated left arm, pretended to look at a watch that was not there, giggled. "Hours. Or minutes. Or . . ." He tilted his head, his exposed eye watering constantly.

"In about ten hours," Jack said. "And the bomb's in the Imperial War Museum."

Miller's one good eye swivelled and settled on Jack. Then he shrugged. "It doesn't matter."

"You're probably right. But what does matter is helping anyone left alive in London. You can do that."

"Me? You see what's left of me, boy? I'm barely human anymore."

"You haven't been human for a long time," Breezer said.

"I'm a scientist, and—"

"You're a murderer!" Breezer stepped forward, and Jack was surprised to see Miller jerk back in his chair. Filled with bravado, still he was in pain, and scared. Good. That might make what came next much easier.

"I'll only ask once," Jack said. "We need you to provide a safe route out of London. We know if we just storm the Exclusion Zone it'll be a massacre. We'll be cut down, bombed, slaughtered. But you can call them off. You can tell the Choppers to stand down and let us out."

"I could," Miller said. "And then all this would be released to the outside world."

"The only thing released would be human beings with remarkable abilities," Jack said. "All this murder and chaos and hatred . . . that's *your* doing."

Miller chuckled again. It shook his body, and his pain was obvious. "I don't care anymore," he said. "I want to die. Look at me! Look what he did to me! My only wish now is for your bastard father to die with me."

"You might want to die," Breezer said, "but what about—"

"You're all monsters," Miller said. "The Evolve was my creation, so you're all my children. And I condemn you to death."

"That's . . ." Breezer shook his head, then looked at Jack.

Jack nodded.

Breezer turned Miller's chair and wedged it against the metal examination table, locking its brakes, holding Miller's one good arm down against the side of the chair. The mutilated man laughed, but Jack could not tell whether he was afraid or purely mad. His remaining, lidless eye was wide open, either way.

"Like father, like son," Miller said.

"No," Jack said. "Not at all."

He stepped forward and pressed his hands to Miller's face.

The same ruins, the same day, the same tumbled wreckage of the London Eye. Lucy-Anne has seen the Eye since her last dream, so this time it is different—less damaged, only scarred high up with the impact site, with charred and broken pods further down where the helicopter tumbled and exploded. The aircraft's blackened remains straddle a safety barrier next to the burnt-out ticket office. Lucy-Anne cannot understand how Angelina Walker survived that wreck to emerge as Nomad. Perhaps she also dreamed herself to life.

As she thinks of her, Nomad appears. She climbs from the helicopter's ruin and jumps down to the ground, landing with barely a touch. She starts to walk away from Lucy-Anne, and it is the dream of destruction once again. In the distance the light will soon bloom, a bright flash that for an instant will look like creation, but will bring destruction.

But Lucy-Anne wonders, *Isn't all creation a violent event? The Big Bang, life from no-life, and London's evolution?*

But there is a difference. The bomb about to erupt is meant purely for destruction, and in its place it will leave a sterile, dead place.

Lucy-Anne follows Nomad, frantically trying to shout for her, but she has no voice. Any time now, any time now . . .

And then Nomad turns back to face her and lifts her hand, points, two fingers aiming at Lucy-Anne like a gun. "You and me," she says. "You and me together." She starts running at Lucy-Anne and the surroundings change in the blink of an eye.

A street, burning, shooting, screaming, bodies, flames and smoke, and Nomad leaps a burning motorbike and drives Lucy-Anne to the ground, straddles her, and drives her pointed fingers down into her throat, silencing the words that were building there—a cry for mercy, a scream of anger, and a question:

You and me?

Lucy-Anne snapped awake and sat up. Sparky held her so she didn't tip to the ground, and Jenna glanced back and smiled. She must only have been asleep for moments, because everything was the same—the ruins of containers and several vehicles, the grotesque scattering of bodies and body parts, and the people she'd come with standing and sitting, waiting for Jack and the man called Breezer to emerge again.

The sun was high and hot. London was warm, but the usual humid, acidic stink of the city was absent now. She could smell only rot and death, and when she blinked she saw Nomad's expressionless face as the woman killed her.

Breezer appeared at the warped door opening in the larger container, stepping out grim-faced. Jack pushed Miller's wheelchair out behind him and let it roll down the ramp on its own. Miller slowed to a halt and looked up at the sky. He looked different. More whole.

"Jack doesn't look too happy," Jenna said.

"Sparky," Lucy-Anne said, holding out her hand. "Help me up, mate. Leg's gone to sleep." He reached for her and held her upright, and she knew that he knew that her leg was fine. She just wanted the contact.

"Your hair needs dyeing again," Sparky said.

"I only did it a week ago." They looked at each other, dumbfounded, as time struck them both. A week ago they'd still been living outside London, ignorant of much that was occurring inside the toxic city, full of rebellion and a need to understand. In her mind her family was still alive, and in Sparky's was the hope that he might see his brother again one day. All those hopes were now dashed, and so much had happened that they were both changed people. They'd never be the same again. Beyond London now seemed as distant and mysterious as the city had once been.

"Fuck me," Sparky whispered.

"Yeah," Lucy-Anne said. She nodded towards Jack.

Jack was gesturing them over. He looked around at the piled containers, alert for trouble. *Probably looking for that Fleeter girl*, Lucy-Anne thought. She'd only known her for an hour or two, but already she didn't like her.

"I've helped him," Jack said. "After all he's done, I healed three broken ribs, eased the pain of his ruptured eye, reset his jaw. I stopped a bleed in his left lung, and dispersed a blood clot that was moving towards his heart." He stood beside Miller and waited until they had gathered around. Only Rhali stayed away at the other side of the clearing. "And I've told him that this is what he'll be destroying. What I can do, and what so many others can do as well."

Miller was shifting in his chair, and at first Lucy-Anne thought he was crying. But then she heard the terrible sound of laughter.

"But he doesn't care," Breezer said.

"Tell him to do what we want!" Sparky said. "That thing Guy Morris could do, you know. Whisper it in his ear! Can't you do that?"

"I tried," Jack said.

Miller's laughter burst into loud, hearty guffaws. He groaned in pain as well, but the discomfort seemed to humour him even more. "Your father would thank you for healing some of what he's done to me," he said. "More for him to torture next time!" His one good eye was rolling in its socket, leaking a pale pink, bloody fluid.

"He's mad," Lucy-Anne said.

"I can belt it out of him," Sparky said, stepping forward with his fist raised.

"No," Lucy-Anne said. "I mean he's really mad. Insane."

Jack nodded. "Maybe that's why I can't get through to him."

Miller looked back over his shoulder at Jack, then at Sparky standing in front of him, fist still raised. "Ohhh, don't hurt me!" he shrieked, cackling, wiping bloody tears from his cheeks.

"Bloody hell," Sparky said. His shoulders slumped.

"So what now?" Lucy-Anne asked.

"Now we all die," Miller said. "Boom! Big Bindy!" He pointed at Lucy-Anne. "You die." He jabbed a finger at Sparky. "Blondie dies." And across at Rhali. "That brown bitch dies, too."

Jack turned to strike him, but he was too late. Lucy-Anne moved quickly, flowing forward and bringing her fist around. She'd always been ready with a punch, even before Doomsday and the strain it had put her under, but this was the first that ever felt truly righteous. She felt the solidity of his cheekbone beneath her knuckles, and heard the creak of his neck as the blow turned his head to the side. It stopped his vile utterances and his laughter, and the silence following the punch was almost peaceful.

"Yeah," Sparky breathed softly.

"Come on," Jack said. "Let's leave him to his bomb. We're getting out of here."

"Leave me?" Miller asked. His voice was fluid with blood. "You're not leaving me. You've saved me." He lifted his right hand and flexed his mended fingers, turning his hand this way and that as if it were something precious. "Oh, thank you, Jack," he said. For the first time, his voice sounded almost normal.

As he reached down into his clothing Lucy-Anne was already moving, pulling Sparky down with her, shouting, "Get down!" Perhaps Jack could have flipped like Fleeter and prevented what happened next. That he didn't could have been down to surprise, or maybe it was something darker. Maybe he really didn't want to.

With the hand Jack had fixed, Miller lifted a gun and pressed its barrel into his mouth. His final mad chuckle was swallowed by the gunshot, and by then Lucy-Anne had looked away. But she still heard the wet patter of Miller's tortured mind scattering across the ground.

There was silence for a few moments. The gunshot echoed away, and somewhere in the distance a flock of birds took startled flight, complaining at the sky.

"Right," Sparky said shakily. "So Miller's probably not going to help us."

Lucy-Anne couldn't hold back a giggle, but it quickly faded. They stood and headed away, all of them doing their best not to look back. Warm wet death was something they had all seen too much of.

Of them all, it was Rhali who walked with the most composure. For the first time since they'd rescued her, she seemed at peace.

They crossed what had once been Camp Hope and passed into the cool shadows between piled containers. When they emerged from the container park and started back towards the river, Lucy-Anne looked around for Andrew. But he was nowhere in sight. She felt a momentary panic, a sense of utter loneliness. Then a hand rested on her shoulder. Rhali.

"Bloody excellent punch," the girl said, grinning from ear to ear.

"Classic!" Sparky said. "I taught her everything she knows!"

"*She* taught *you*, more like," Jenna said.

"I was always scared of her," Jack said. "It's the purple hair, I think."

Lucy-Anne gave Jack the finger. "Eat me."

Her old boyfriend raised one eyebrow, and Sparky started making some rude gestures behind his back.

Lucy-Anne laughed a little. And she also cried gentle, thankful tears, because she was back with her friends, and they were as close to family as she had left anywhere in the world.

Keen to get away from Camp H and the horrors it still contained, they decided to cruise upriver again towards where they had embarked. There was the silent understanding that they had talking to do and decisions to make, but for now putting distance between them and the camp was the priority.

Fleeter had not reappeared. Jack said she was probably following them, and that made Lucy-Anne uncomfortable. But at the same time she was returning to herself, feeling stronger, and grasping a new purpose—to help her friends survive.

"Are you sure they won't just let us out?" Lucy-Anne asked Jack. They were sitting in the open at the boat's bow, watching the serene Thames ahead of them awaiting the boat's disturbing wash. The others were under cover back towards the cabin. Jack looked sad and lost.

"They've kept everyone in London for this long," Jack said. "I've heard plenty of stories about escapees being murdered. Bodies put on display, sometimes, to dissuade others from trying to break out. Why would they change their minds now? Their problem of London is about to be solved once and for all, so they'll do more than ever to keep anyone from getting out."

"But they'll be retreating," Lucy-Anne said. "Pulling back, if they know what's about to happen."

"Not until the last minute, I doubt. They'll have trucks, helicopters." He shook his head.

"It's not hopeless," she said, sensing the despair in him. He only looked at her. "Really!" she insisted. "We've got nine, ten hours yet. We'll find a way."

"I don't see how," he said. Lucy-Anne reached out and held his hand, and a rush of memories of her and Jack assaulted her. Most of them were good. He was above all her friend.

"We stop the bomb or get out," she said. "Anything else is not an option." She was proud of herself. Saying that whilst remembering her dreams—the blast, the flames, the heat-flash blanching everything that London had become into a white-hot mess—took some effort.

Jack smiled, then sat back against the bench. "We thought we'd lost you," he said. "So what happened?"

"Rook found me," she said. She leaned back next to Jack, and with the sun on her face and the gentle movements of the boat, she felt almost relaxed. London could almost have been its old self again.

"A Superior," Jack said.

"No, not at all. Rook was all on his own. He went with Reaper because it suited his purpose."

"Which was?"

"Revenge. He was in a dark place. Such a . . . sensitive boy. He and his brother survived Doomsday and lived together for a while, but then the Choppers took his brother, and the birds showed him what happened. They slaughtered him. Took his brain."

"They've experimented on so many," Jack said.

"But he saw something in me. We connected, I guess. And

maybe fell for each other, just a little." It seemed strange talking like this with Jack, because until recently they had been a couple. But she sensed no hostility from him, and no surprise. Their relationship had been strong from the moment they'd met, marred only by the weight of expectation between them—that they should be together. They were much better together as friends. Anything else just got in the way.

"I saved him," she said. She sensed Jack's confusion.

"I thought he was gone?"

"He is, now. But I thought I'd saved him. I've got something too."

"The dreaming? Nomad touched you?"

"I've met her, Jack. Seen her in my dreams, and met her for real, and sometimes both are the same. But the thing I've got is all my own. Something I've always had, when I think back to when I was younger, but always a more subtle thing than it is now. More gentle. Nomad told me I was what she's been looking for forever. And Rook too, he told me his brother had something of his gift even before Doomsday."

"So what does that mean? And what can you do?"

"I think it might mean that everyone left alive had something beforehand that Evolve caught onto. And I can dream. At first I thought I was seeing the future, or forms it might take. I dreamed of meeting Rook and his birds attacking me, and they did, briefly, after he died. I dreamed of Nomad and the bomb. I dreamed of meeting you by the river and the Choppers waiting there, but I didn't know how that one turned out, and didn't have a chance to change it."

"Change?"

"I think I can . . . I thought I could change events in my dreams. Lucid dreaming, guiding things. Rook died and I dreamed him alive again, and for a while he was." She looked at the scratches on the back of her hand, put there by Rook's nails as he fell into the hole. "But then fate caught up with him, exactly as I'd seen it before. I might have stretched things a little, but I don't think I really changed anything."

"That's amazing," Jack said. "I had nothing before. Don't think so, anyway. But Nomad's touch has given me . . ." He trailed off, looking into a distance no one else could see.

"What?" Lucy-Anne asked.

"So much," he said. "So much that I really don't know what I might become."

"So we're special," Lucy-Anne said. She couldn't keep the bitterness from her voice, because being special hadn't done much for her thus far. "My talent's not caused by Doomsday, and it's grown just by being here. And you've been touched by a freak."

"We're *all* special," Jack said, looking along the boat at his friends. Rhali smiled. Sparky gave them the finger. "Differentiating between who has a gift and who doesn't—who's normal, or Irregular, or Superior—loses sight of everyone's uniqueness. We do that, and we might as well sink the boat and drown right now."

Lucy-Anne thought of Rook and how conflicted his gift had made him. She'd seen him cold-bloodedly killing Choppers out of a burning need for revenge. She had also seen his more vulnerable, needy side, and the part of him that was still a child. And she realised that the Rook she'd fallen for had been the human boy, nothing more or less.

"We're all special," she said, nodding.

"And we always were."

"So we stop the bomb or get out." She smiled at Jack, her special friend. "Sinking the boat is not an option."

"Right." He smiled back. For a moment too brief to measure but too precious to ignore, all was well with the world.

CHAPTER EIGHT NINE

"On the bridge," Sparky said. "I'd recognise that spooky bastard anywhere."

Jack turned and looked ahead of them, certain he was about to see his father again and unsure what he thought about that. He felt sick and excited. Outwardly he'd disowned him—Reaper was a murderer and exuded little hope of redemption. Inside, Jack still remembered the kind man he used to love so much.

But it was not Reaper standing in the centre of Tower Bridge looking down at the approaching boat.

"Puppeteer," Lucy-Anne said. She more than anyone had cause to remember him; he'd almost killed her back in that hotel, just before the Choppers arrived and everything went to hell.

"Thought we'd seen the last of them," Jenna said.

"What shall I do?" Breezer sounded scared, and Jack could not blame him. Any time the Superiors intruded in their lives, it meant that either they wanted something, or that things were about to get much worse. Perhaps both.

"Carry on," Jack said. "Let's see what happens." He looked around the boat, trying to make out whether Fleeter was with them or not. He thought she'd gone, but it was possible that she'd come along for the ride, sitting quietly flipped out. Twenty minutes on the river for them would have felt like twelve hours for her, but she was inscrutable. He had no idea what her aims were.

"I'm going to see if Fleeter's with us," he said. Sparky and Jenna nodded.

"What do you—?" Lucy-Anne began.

"Blink and I'll be back," he said. He leaned closer to her. "Trust me."

Lucy-Anne grinned. It was her cheeky, mischievous grin that he'd fallen for, and he felt a moment of nostalgia for the time they'd spent as an item.

Then he closed his eyes and grasped the talent, and before anyone spoke again he flipped.

The impact of changing his pace with the world thumped him in the gut and chest. He opened his eyes and looked around, and for a moment he knew he could take a breath. The world took on that surreal, deadened sheen he'd already become used to, and everything was still . . . almost. There was movement all around, but because it was barely noticeable it felt like a fluid, dizzying sensation. He could not see anything moving. But everything was.

Fleeter was nowhere to be seen.

His friends on the boat were stuck where he'd left them. Breezer drove, eyes dead ahead. And Lucy-Anne looked at him with wide, fluid eyes. If he could wait here motionless for long enough, he'd see her eyes growing wider and her mouth falling open as she realised that he'd gone. But even here, out of phase with the world, the clock was ticking.

He quickly scanned the bridge ahead of them and the shores on either side, looking for any other signs of Superiors being present. He couldn't believe that Puppeteer's presence was an accident, nor that he was here on his own. The tall man stood at the decorative railing, hands on the handrail, leaning slightly out and looking down at their boat. There was no one else on the bridge, but he saw a silhouette on one of the bridge's wide stone feet that might have been another person. He leaned left and right, trying to get a better view, but they were hidden in shadow.

If Fleeter was close by, she'd likely see that he'd flipped. And then she would either hide or come to him. He called her name. His voice was flat and dead against the motionless air, and it probably didn't carry very far.

Jack glanced at Puppeteer one more time, and his pose suggested that he was about to raise his hands. He seemed coiled. Jack frowned. Something was going to happen, and he had to be ready as soon as he flipped back.

He could not put off the future forever.

Lucy-Anne was still staring at him, and her gasp of shock came upon his return.

"Where . . ."

"I sped up, that's all. Or slowed everything else down." He frowned. "Not really sure how it works exactly."

"Let's save that for later," Jenna said. "Look." She pointed up at the bridge, where Puppeteer had raised his hands into claws.

"Okay then," Jack said. He stood at the bow of the boat. "Breezer!" he called back over his shoulder. "Aim for the central span."

"What're you going to do?" Lucy-Anne asked.

Jack breathed deeply and heard Sparky say, "Magic!" Then he felt the air close all around him as if holding him in a fist, and his right foot left the boat's deck.

Rhali called out in alarm. Jenna and Sparky grabbed a leg each. Jack relaxed his mind, and then reached out with Puppeteer's own power.

He actually felt the tall man's clothing and skin against his palms. He lifted, his strength incredible, and as he brought Puppeteer out over the bridge's edge he felt himself drop to the deck again. The Superior had lost his hold.

"Yeah!" Sparky said.

Jack let go. Puppeteer fell and splashed into the Thames fifty feet ahead of them.

Jack relaxed, biting his lip to see away the brief dizziness that accompanied his use of a powerful talent. *Is that the first sign of the sickness?* he wondered. But he could not concern himself with that. In the scheme of things it was insignificant.

Puppeteer was splashing in the river's embrace, and Sparky heaved a lifebelt overboard. "Don't pollute the river!" he shouted.

"Jack! On the bridge!" Jenna pointed, and Jack already knew what he was going to see. More Superiors. Shade was there, barely visible between blinks, and the sleek form of Scryer rushing along the pavement. Of Reaper there was no sign.

"What do you want?" Jack shouted at Puppeteer. The man was clasping the lifebelt now, drifting past them in the grip of the river's flow. He stared back at Jack but gave no sign of having heard.

Jack reached out and clasped him, lifted him from the river, higher, higher, and even though he felt Puppeteer pushing back with his power, Jack was much stronger. When he was almost as high as the bridge again Jack let go and he fell, crying out slightly before striking the Thames once more. He disappeared beneath the surface then quickly popped up again, gasping, splashing around as he sought the dropped lifebelt. But he had drifted behind their boat now, and every second put more distance between them.

"What is this?" Jack shouted. Puppeteer turned away and started kicking for shore.

"I'm not happy going under there," Breezer called from the cabin. They were closing on the bridge supports now, and the shadow Jack had seen underneath was no longer there.

"No choice," he said. "Get us through as fast as you can."

"I haven't seen Reaper," Sparky said.

"No," Jack said. "But I've got a feeling we'll be seeing him soon."

Lucy-Anne was kneeling at the boat's bow like some slinky figurehead, and she pointed beneath the bridge. "Look! What the hell is *she* doing?"

Jack recognised the silhouette and the pose, and his heart sank.

The woman was inhaling and exhaling quickly, so hard that they could hear her breaths from two hundred feet away. And the surface of the slow-moving river was changing. Its texture altered, and it started glimmering even within the shadow cast by the great bridge.

"Better ease up," Jack called to Breezer.

"Why?"

"'Cos this boat's not built for ice breaking." As Breezer eased back on the throttle and their momentum carried them against the flow, the woman froze the river beneath the bridge's widest span. The surface became slushy at first, and then quickly grew into harder ridges, grinding against each other as the currents beneath played with the chunks of ice. Some of them parted from the mass and started drifting downriver, and they impacted gently against the boat's bow.

"If you want to talk, why don't you just say?" Jack shouted. The ice woman continued breathing hard, and for a few seconds he thought no one was going to reply.

But then he heard his father's voice. "Where's the fun in that?"

Reaper appeared from beneath the bridge and walked out onto the river. He stepped from one block of ice to another, balancing confidently on the moving mass, and came towards the boat. Shade was with him, seeming to form shadows where none should be.

"Your puppet guy's become a floater," Sparky said. Reaper did not even respond. He was staring only at Jack, and Jack knew that he had already disregarded everyone else.

The boat nudged against the expanding slew of ice, and the ice woman kept breathing, solidifying the ice floe so that it barely moved beneath the river's drift. Jack could not conceive of the energies required to do that, but he did blink into his own universe and find the star that would give him the power. He shivered, and his next breath condensed in the air before him.

"We don't want you on our boat," Jack said.

Reaper raised an eyebrow. "I didn't ask your permission." He reached up to the boat's handrail and grabbed hold, ready to board.

Without thinking, Jack growled. The ice floe shook and cracked with several loud reports, and the ice woman paused, surprised, to watch.

Reaper stepped back from the boat, arms out to maintain his balance as the ice moved beneath him.

"That's not polite," he said.

"Piss on you," Jack said. He had never, ever spoken to his father like that before. But this man was not his father. He might resemble him slightly, and some of the mannerisms were the same. But Jack had seen and heard too much of what he could do to feel any true connection.

"That's *definitely* not polite. Shade?"

Jack clasped inward, and became like Shade. He shifted while barely touching the space he passed, taking any hint of shadows to himself as camouflage, squeezing through hollows in the air and meeting Shade head-on as he tried to board the boat.

"I . . . said . . . *no*!" Jack injected that last word with another taste of his father's own power. Shade was thrown across the ice to land on his back, sliding quickly into the shadow of a small ice ridge and standing, waiting, the shock evident on his face.

Jack drew back to himself.

"I don't want to fight you, Dad."

"Because you know you'll lose."

"Because I know *you'll* lose. And I don't want that on my conscience."

"So just what the hell do you want?" Jenna asked Reaper, trying to defuse the growing pressure. "No Choppers here for you to torture and kill. Perhaps you're after us now?"

"No," Reaper sighed, "I'm not after you. Not to torture and kill, and least."

"Then why?" Jack asked. "And hurry. We're in a rush."

"A rush? Why? Anyone would think there's a clock ticking somewhere." Reaper stepped further back from the boat so that he could see everyone on board, and even before it happened Jack felt a warning niggle, a suspicion that he'd relaxed just a little too much. Perhaps pride was a factor, because he had seen off Puppeteer and Shade, and even Reaper seemed unsettled.

But he forgot that Reaper was a monster.

A single cough from the man who'd been his father thundered across the boat. Timber stretched and splintered, the glassed-in area shattered, and Jack was lifted from his feet and thrown back into the rows of benches. He heard the others crying out, and he saw Rhali with her hands pressed to her stomach, winded, eyes wide as she tried to catch her breath. Blood ran across his scalp, and pain bit into his right hip and shoulder. Anger flushed through him. Talents flickered before him, all of them powerful and destructive. He could have breathed out and set the boat on fire, or punched at the air and launched a compression wave that would crush metal. But he sensed also that this was a defining moment in his relationship with his new, wider universe of potential. If he let go to anger, chaos would reign.

So he remained on the deck while Reaper climbed aboard, and

Shade flowed over the handrail, and the ice woman breathed out again, frosting the remains of glass in the boat's viewing area and freezing the hull to the spreading ice.

With a *crack!* Fleeter appeared on the bridge support. She hurried across the ice and climbed onto the boat, glancing around to assess the situation. She grinned at Jack, but he did not return her smile.

"Bastard," Sparky said. He was on his knees, fists clenched and ready to lash out at Reaper, and Jack had to grasp his ankle. His friend looked back at him. Jack shook his head.

"*Now* can we talk?" Reaper asked.

Sparky stood anyway, and Shade flitted across the deck towards him. Sparky threw a punch but it hit only air, and then he was flipped onto his back, the wind knocked from him.

"I'd prefer you all stayed lying down," Reaper said. "Less chance of trouble that way. Less chance of any of you getting hurt." He stared at Jack when he said this.

"You'll hurt us anyway," Jack said. "It's in your nature."

"To be honest, Jack, you've taught me a thing or two," Reaper said. He nodded at Breezer, leaning against the smashed wheelhouse nursing a bleeding hand and a gashed cheek. "It used to be that I regarded people like him with disdain. Loathing, even. Given a gift, they do nothing with it. They let it fester and stew, and they exist apart from what they were given, not as a part of it. You can't separate yourself from your true natures. You of all people should know that now."

"This was forced upon me," Jack said.

"Me also! But I relish it." He walked forward and sat on a bench, almost within reach of Jack. "Tell me you don't relish what you have, too."

Jack did not answer.

"You feel the power. You know you're different, and better than everyone else." He waved a hand to indicate Sparky and the others. Behind Reaper, Fleeter was still smiling. Jack bristled.

"Different, yes. Very different. I've got abilities now . . . I could crush you with a blink." He knelt up, and then stood, taller than his sitting father. Holding out his hand, he felt the heat-rush of a new star. "I could clasp your heart and halt its beat," Jack said with wonder. "I could get into your head and destroy your sense of self. Make you . . . a robot. A hollow man."

Reaper sat up straighter, his cruel face taking on its usual anger.

"Before you could even think about muttering one of your earthquake whispers," Jack said, "I could heat your guts to the temperature of the sun and melt you where you sit."

"Then do it," Reaper breathed.

"No," Jack said. "Because you're right. I am different from all my friends. But I'm no better than any of them. I'm using what I have . . . I'm doing my best to help people. Not crush them. Not kill them."

"But you've killed before," Reaper said, smiling.

Jack glanced up at Fleeter, and she looked away. Her smile slipped. Was that shame, or fear?

"Yes, she's been watching you for me. And yes, she saw you dispatch those three Choppers. Imagine their families now, Jack. A little son waiting to see his father again. A daughter, returning from school with a picture she's painted for Mummy. Except Mummy isn't coming home. Because you turned her into jam."

"I *have* imagined, and I always will. And it hurts. Because I care and you don't, and that makes you . . ." Jack shook his head, angry, shaking with frustration. "Worthless! You're worthless, Dad. You have so much, and you mean so little." He sighed. "It's really so, so sad."

Reaper stood. Jack tensed, but sensed no violence brewing in the man. Not yet. But he remained ready, each fingertip touching a different star. He *thrummed* with power, and he knew that if Reaper or any of the other Superiors made an aggressive move, he'd sweep them all away.

He wouldn't kill them. He'd simply move them aside so that he and his friends could carry on. Stronger than he had ever been before, his greatest strength was understanding his place. A friend amongst friends. Special, but no more than them.

"Go, Dad," he said.

"Come with us," Reaper said. It still sounded more like an order than a request. "No one can stop the bomb, so we're going to break out. And with your help, we'll succeed."

"Just me?" Jack asked.

"*All* of you." Reaper glanced around the boat, never looking at anyone for long. He only really had eyes for Jack.

"What is this?" Jack asked. He laughed, looked at Fleeter, but she was silent. "Just what? Last time we met you were happy to stay here and torture what you left of Miller. You wanted only violence, even when the Irregulars and Superiors did have some kind of alliance. So what is this?"

"A new alliance to save us all," Reaper said.

"You don't need a healer, or a truth seer, to break out of London," Jack said. "You've got all the firepower you need."

Reaper stared at Jack as if trying to will the truth his way. But Jack still did not understand.

"We've chosen our own paths," Jack said at last. "We're going to find a peaceful way out, for everyone. You and your so-called Superiors can do what you want."

"But they're trying to kill us all!" Reaper said, and it was the closest Jack had heard him sound vulnerable and desperate. It was a plea.

But Jack looked around the boat at his friends, and he sensed their silent support.

"And that's why we'll escape London with the moral high ground," he said. "Slaughter a thousand Choppers to get out, lose hundreds more survivors to the machine guns, and what way is that to expose ourselves to the world? People are going to be frightened enough of us. We have to show that we mean no harm."

"And get blown up in the process," Reaper said. "Very dignified. Very honourable."

"Perhaps," Jack said.

Reaper seemed ready to say something more, but he shook his head instead.

"You'll see that our way is the only way," Jack said. "Use violence to break out, and they'll stop you eventually. Lock you up. Cut you into pieces, kill you."

"You think we're destined for anything else?" Reaper asked, almost defeated.

"Tell them," Fleeter said. The moment froze, as if the ice woman had gasped and chilled the air.

"Tell us what?" Jack asked.

Fleeter seemed nervous, shifting from foot to foot. Her smile remained, and Jack realised that it was a natural part of her. It displayed neither humour nor mockery, but rather a grim acceptance of how things were.

"Reaper," she said. "Tell them why you really want the Irregulars with you."

Reaper glared at her.

"A distraction," she said. She took a couple of steps towards Jack, a symbolic gesture that seemed to shift the whole balance on the boat. *I still can't trust her for a second*, Jack thought. But this was more confusing than ever. Was it a part of Reaper's play?

"You can leave with him," Jack said.

"Yeah, get the hell off my boat," Sparky said.

Fleeter shook her head and came closer to Jack. He readied himself to flip, and at the first sign of her going he would do so. He wouldn't let her phase out, grasp him, knock him out, put him down. Everyone was depending on him, and that idea had been growing for some time. He was no better than any of them—he believed that deeply, because humility had always been a part of him—but they did rely on him. In these dangerous times, his own deadliness was their protection.

"You're cannon fodder," Fleeter said to Jack. "You and all the Irregulars. Cause a distraction, draw fire while we can . . . while Reaper and the Superiors can escape."

Jack saw Reaper tense, and then smile again. "Jack could have found that out for himself, I'm sure," he said. "Asked me a question with one power." He wiggled his fingers like a manic spider. "Delved inside my mind with another."

"I chose not to," Jack said. Fleeter paused, slightly closer to him than Reaper. She was waiting for the violence her revelation might bring, or perhaps some sign of acceptance from Jack. She received neither.

"It doesn't matter," Reaper said. He nodded at Fleeter. "*You* don't matter. We'll still be ready when you are. Make your own ineffectual efforts to get out, and we'll be right behind you."

"If I thought there was an ounce of decency left in you, I'd ask you to be with us," Jack said.

Reaper chuckled softly, and the ice flow trapping the boat

rumbled and cracked. "But there's not," he said. He glanced up at the sun. "Nine, maybe eight hours left. And while we wait for you weaklings to make your move, there are still Choppers left to hunt." With that he turned and jumped from the boat, and Shade and the ice woman followed.

Jack could have stopped them. For a moment he even saw what might happen—the ice cracking in great convulsions, rearing up, smashing together with Reaper and his other Superiors trapped between the solid slabs, and then flowing quickly along the Thames. Anyone not crushed to death would drown. Anyone not drowned would be slaughtered by the Choppers stationed at the Thames barrier.

He knew he could do it. But the moment when he considered that was over in a blink, and then Fleeter was sitting before him, almost contrite.

"Right," she said. "Right. Okay. I've just pissed off Reaper."

"I do it all the time," Jack said.

The others around the boat rose and sat on benches, nursing cuts and bruises and breathing a collective sigh of relief.

"Intense," Sparky said. "London is just way too intense for me. Give me a little village, country lanes, forests, a pub."

"Maybe soon," Lucy-Anne said, and for a while no one said anything else.

Maybe soon, Jack thought. But for the life of him he didn't know how.

Fleeter sat on her own at the bow of the boat. Jack tended to Breezer—healing his wounds, easing the bruising he'd received across his left shoulder as he'd fallen—and then he moved up close to Fleeter to try and clear the ice. She looked ahead, beneath the bridge, even though he was close behind her. Either something about her had changed radically, or she was a good actress.

Jack leaned over the handrail and dipped both hands into the cold water. The ice was already turning slushy without the ice woman there to tend it, and as Jack heated the water from one of his inner suns, the boat drifted away from the floe's grasp. Breezer started the engine and reversed the boat, aiming for the gentle arch closer to the north bank.

Jack sat close to Fleeter and looked back at the others. They were sitting close, talking quietly, tending cuts and bruises and trying to move on from the tense confrontation. Rhali more than anyone seemed quite calm, but she had not seen what Reaper could do. And what she had been through was worse than anything he could have dreamed up.

"So," Jack said.

He heard Fleeter laugh softly, but they sat almost back to back. He knew that sometimes it was easier to speak honestly when you did not have to look someone in the face.

"So," Fleeter said, "Reaper was telling the truth. I've been following you ever since I got back from taking your mother and sister out of London. And though a big part of why I did so was because Reaper asked me, because he likes control and, well, I think somewhere inside he still cares a little . . . I also followed you for myself."

Jack wasn't sure what she meant. She'd flirted with him, but he'd put it down to her seeking a measure of control more than anything else. "For yourself?" he asked.

She laughed again, and this time it sounded more heartfelt. "Don't flatter yourself. Well, maybe you're a cutie, Jack. Maybe you are. But I know you've got a good heart, and you've seen what I can do, and what I've done. I know you're still beating yourself up about those Choppers you had to kill. I must be a monster to you."

"No," Jack began, but Fleeter turned around and grabbed his shoulder, hard enough to hurt. She pulled him around to face her. She was serious. Even behind the omnipresent smile, she was as serious as he'd ever seen her.

"I saw outside," she said. Her eyes went wide like a kid seeing Disneyworld for the first time. "When I took them through there was a sense of . . . release. Even though there were still houses and streets where we came out, it all felt so different. It felt like another world because it *was* another world, and I knew that. And for the first time in a long while I allowed myself to . . . to remember."

She trailed off, but Jack did not prompt her. This was a story she had to tell in her own time.

"Almost as soon as Doomsday happened, my life became a dream," she said. "I've always been a daydreamer. When I was a kid my mother said I'd sit in the garden with my dolls and plastic animals and . . . just . . . disappear. Into my own world. She told me she used to worry about it, but then she started seeing it as something wonderful. I'd sit there for hours just playing, totally immersed in my imagination, and those dolls and animals would come to life. She timed me once, and I was there for almost three hours without looking up. And when I did look up she said I looked blank, blinking, wondering where I was. Then I smiled at her . . . at my mummy . . . and . . ."

There were tears in her eyes, but she seemed unaware.

"Guiding your mother and Emily out of London reminded me of the world I've forgotten," she said. "Reaper took me in and made me what I am." She frowned, shook her head. "No. He showed me the way. What I became was all my fault. But under his wing I forgot my mother and my brother, and London became my whole world. Coming back in yesterday, leaving your mother and sister out there, free, in the world I've forgotten . . . that made me realise I've been living in a dream. For the last two years, with Reaper and the others, doing what I do and seeing what I've seen. All of it has been a dream."

"And you're waking up," Jack said.

"No, Jack," Fleeter said. "But at least I *know* I'm dreaming. Helping you get back to your family, helping you all . . . perhaps that'll give me a chance to wake."

Jack could have asked Breezer to use his own talent to probe inward, discover Fleeter's truths. And Jack thought he could have also done so himself. But he thought this was something that demanded trust.

"Thank you," he said, and he meant it.

"Don't thank me yet." She shrugged. "I know he's your father, and there's more of that left in him than you give him credit for. But Reaper's a mean bastard. No saying what he'll do next."

"Yeah, I know," Jack said. "Not as if we haven't already got stuff keeping us on our toes."

She laughed again, and Jack prodded her shoulder, a friendly nudge. He might have hit Sparky in the same way. Something told him that Fleeter was not the hugging kind.

CHAPTER NINE
EIGHT

They moored the boat and disappeared into an Italian restaurant on the riverfront, gathering in the kitchen, and their mood was dour. Few words were exchanged. They had to formulate a plan, but their futures looked so bleak that no one knew where to begin.

Breezer decided to leave. Jack asked him to stay, but he only shook his head, defeated. "I have friends," he said. "People who've looked up to me for too long for me to abandon them now. I want to be with them when . . . at the end."

"You can't just give up!" Jack said.

"*You* can't," Breezer replied. "Jack, you can get your friends out easily. With the abilities you have, and with her." He nodded at Fleeter. She sat apart from the others, quiet and still.

"There's no way I'll do that and leave everyone else to die," Jack said. But the harsh idea had already crossed his mind. Around eight hours until the bomb exploded, and soon would come the cut-off time for him and the others to escape London. Before then they'd have a chance, and Breezer was right—Jack could get them out. After that point, they'd have run out of time to flee. He didn't know the extent of the damage the bomb would cause, but the Exclusion Zone formed the boundary they had to cross.

The thought of running, and failing everyone in London, was terrible. Jack's abilities gave him a sense of responsibility which he couldn't shake. When the time came, perhaps he would send Fleeter out with his friends. But he could never leave. Nomad's touch had made him a part of what London had become, whether that city's doom was sealed or not.

"We can't just give up," he said to Breezer. This time it sounded like a plea. The others were watching, and Jenna stood close to Jack, supporting him with her strong silence.

"We rush the Exclusion Zone, they cut us down," Breezer said. "We stay here, we're toast."

"Something will happen," Jack said. "I'll *make* something happen. See the truth in what I say. It's what you do, so see it!"

Breezer sighed, eyelids drooping. "I see that you *want* it to be the truth," he said. "You're a good kid, Jack."

"So don't just sit down and die!" Jack said. "You've already spread the word to get as many as you can to Heron Tower. So now go back there and take them west."

"And then?" Breezer asked.

"One way or another, we'll march out of London. And if we have to fight our way out, so be it. Better than just waiting for the bomb."

Breezer sighed, nodded. He seemed relieved to have had the weight of decision taken from his own shoulders.

"Good luck," Breezer said. He shook Jack's hand. "You and your friends . . . you're pretty amazing. I'll see you in the west. We'll wait somewhere near Chiswick."

"I'll find you."

As Breezer left, Jack eased himself down against a metal cabinet and sighed. He was exhausted, and the universe inside seemed to be thrumming with expectation. The whole of his world knew that something momentous and terrible was about to occur.

"So now what?" Sparky asked at last. "It's a mess. We're lost."

"We're doing everything we can," Jenna said, but even she no longer sounded certain and strong. Jack heard her doubts, and when Rhali sat close beside him, he leaned into her and smiled.

"Fleeter," Jack said. "Any thoughts?"

"Only that we should get out of London."

"And leave everyone else to die."

She did not reply, but she looked troubled.

"Lucy-Anne?" Jenna asked.

"I can dream," Lucy-Anne said. She sounded far away, talking to herself. "When I'm dreaming, and I know I'm there, I can move things as I want. Make things happen as I want them to happen. But I don't think *I'm* really in charge. Maybe it's fate. Perhaps I can just . . . juggle fate, for a little while."

"What do you mean?" Jack asked.

"I've dreamed of the bomb," Lucy-Anne said. "I see Nomad and then the bomb explodes. Except . . ." She frowned.

"Lucy-Anne?" Jenna prompted.

"Except now it's mixed up with another dream. I see Nomad, and she kills me."

"We can't just stop an atom bomb with a bloody dream!" Sparky said.

Lucy-Anne didn't seem to hear him. She was frowning, lost in her own world, and Jack went to her and touched her chin. Her tears were cool. He lifted her face.

"We'll do whatever we can," he said. "And with everything that's happened, I do believe a dream can help. I do."

She smiled past her sadness and loss.

"Eight hours," Jack said, turning around to face the others. "Four hours to do whatever we can to stop the bomb or find a safe way out. And then if none of that works, we go west, meet Breezer and the others, and try to get out anyway. What do you think?"

No one replied, but everyone nodded. As plans went, it was woolly. But it was all they had.

Moving north towards the Thames, Andrew saw a man about to die.

The man was wearing no uniform, yet he had the bearing of a military man—cropped hair, slim build, a neat moustache. He carried no weapons. If he had, there was a chance they might have saved him from what was about to kill him. But even then, Andrew thought it unlikely.

The creature circled him. It had been human once, and though still retaining some vestiges of humanity in appearance, its actions and movements were alien. Taller than the man and thinner, its legs long and chitinous, torso human-sized but covered entirely in a sleek, shiny shell, it was its head that still reflected humanity—human eyes, long hair, a head longer and thinner yet still recognisable.

It clicked and snicked, circled the man, drooled.

The man was begging, and it was his words that drew Andrew into the confrontation. Any other time he would have moved away, not even turning when the screams and noises began. Those inhuman creatures did not concern him, because they could always sense that he too was no longer wholly human. And he knew that even they found him troubling.

"I can stop it!" the man said. "Please, please!" He was panicked, verging on hysterical. Andrew wondered where he came from.

"Stop what?" Andrew said. He crossed the road and stood on a traffic island, ten steps away from the desperate man. The creature only glanced at Andrew before seeming to disregard him.

"The bomb!" the man said. He gasped when he looked at Andrew, uncertain that he was even there.

"You're normal," Andrew said. "You're not one of us."

The man uttered a sharp, insane laugh. "What the hell *is* it? What the hell are *you*?"

"How can you stop the bomb?"

The man's shirt was soaked through with sweat, and he carried a small rucksack over one shoulder, grasping the strap as if it was precious.

"Because it's what I was sent in to do," he said.

"So you're one of them," Andrew said. "One of the people keeping London hidden away as a dirty, dark secret."

"Do you blame us?" he asked, nodding at the creature scratching sharp claws across the road surface.

"Yes," Andrew said. "Completely. But if you can stop the bomb, perhaps you amongst all of them can redeem yourself, a little."

"That's what I want," the man said. "I lost an uncle and three cousins to Doomsday. All dead, not . . . changed. Not like you. And when we heard that madman Miller had triggered the countdown, I was one of the first to volunteer to come in. Deactivate it."

Andrew moved towards the man, passing the creature and sensing the startling intelligence its appearance seemed to belie. The man cringed back a little, but not too far. He seemed used to the strangeness that London now harboured. Though he had never seen anything like Andrew. "So what happened?" Andrew asked.

"We were attacked. The Superiors. Only three of us got away, and we hid, discussed what to do. And we decided . . . between us . . . to carry on." He touched his jacket. "Tried to dress more normally. There was no talking to them! No reasoning! They attacked us, but did they know what we were coming to do? Do you think they even had a clue?"

"So what happened to the other two?" Andrew asked, ignoring the question. He knew about Superiors. They would have attacked the Choppers without pause, and without mercy. Killing those who might, this time, save them.

"We split up. I lost touch with them this morning." The man took a phone from his pocket.

"Let me hear," Andrew said. The man did something to the device and then hesitantly held it out. Andrew closed his eyes and listened.

The hollow, low moan of eternity. Andrew had heard it when he died, and the sound haunted him now, as if mocking his unnatural state and assuring him that, soon, he would be where he belonged. There was a sickening sense of scope to that noise, as if it was the underlying note to an infinite universe, nothing to echo from, its travel never-ending. If Andrew had possessed a body he would have shuddered.

"They're both dead," he said, opening his eyes.

"And . . . you?" the man asked.

Andrew simply stared at him.

The creature scuttled forward and Andrew turned, insubstantial hands held out. "No! He's important," he said. "You came down from the north because of the bomb, and he might be able to stop it."

The thing darted closer, mandibles gaping, wet mouth already working as if chewing at flesh. The man gasped and pressed back against a wall, and Andrew stepped in front of the creature.

It skidded to a stop, scarring the road.

"He's important," Andrew said again, quieter. He urged the man along the pavement, backing away from the creature. He could not tell whether it heard him at all, and if so whether it understood.

"Which way?" the man whispered.

"Whichever way looks best," Andrew said. "But slowly. Don't give it the opportunity of a fast hunt. Might like that."

"Oh, great. Great." The man whispered. "And now I'm listening to a ghost."

The creature watched them go. Andrew smiled. He'd experienced a frisson of fear, and it had been good to feel human again. But the fear had not been for himself.

After a few minutes they passed a multi-storey car park, and the man stepped inside. He paused between ranks of forgotten vehicles, hands on his knees, leaning over as if about to be sick.

"You need to stay with me," Andrew said.

"A dead guy. You're coming with me to the museum?"

"No. You're coming with me away from it."

"No," the man said, shaking his head. "No, no, I have to go where the bomb is."

"Go there alone and you'll die," Andrew said. "You think the thing that almost ate you was strange? Wait until you reach the museum. There are scores of them there. They've come down from the north, and none of them can do anything to prevent what's going to happen."

"But *I* can!" the man shouted. "So they'll let me pass, let me in!"

"Like the Superiors did?" Andrew shook his head. "They're different now. Moved on. Evolved. Just because you and they want the same thing, don't assume they won't eat you."

The man closed his eyes and grabbed his hair in despair.

"But I've got an idea," Andrew said.

"We don't have time for ideas!"

"We'll have time for this one." He circled the man, trying to exude confidence, calmness. "What's your name?"

"Hayden."

"Hayden . . . that Range Rover. See it? Wait in there and I'll bring people who will help."

"What people?"

Andrew thought of his sweet sister. "Special people. Now hide yourself away and stay safe. Right now you might be the most important person in London."

"I've got to try," Jack said. "I've got to try!"

"We'll keep watch," Sparky said, and he and Jenna slipped from the kitchen and out into the restaurant area. Jack guessed they'd like some time on their own. Rhali stayed with him in the kitchen, but her eyelids were drooping, and she fell quickly asleep.

"What do you think you can do?" Lucy-Anne asked.

"I know so much of what I can do already," he said. "But there has to be something more. Something that can help us. All I have to do is . . ." He pretend-grabbed something from the air and clasped his fist shut, staring at it, knuckles white with pressure.

"Not your fault if you can't," Fleeter said.

"Maybe not," Jack said. "But I've got to look for something. I feel the weight."

"Of responsibility," Lucy-Anne said. "Yeah. I think we all feel something of that."

Jack smiled at his friend and then at Fleeter, pleased that the girl smiled back. She was changing, slowly. The problem was they no longer had time for slow.

"Won't be long," Jack said to all of them, and then he sat in a corner between units and closed his eyes.

He fell into his universe. He was a shooting star, a fleeting spark of hope. Infinity was nothing because he had infinite speed, and he moved from one talent to the next. At first he touched abilities he was already familiar with—a shout like Reaper's, Rhali's sense of movement, Fleeter's flexing of time and movement. He gathered them to him and let them go again, comforted by their familiarity. Then he moved on to other stars, reaching out with hopeful fingers.

He could pass through walls, manipulating the quirks and quarks of quantum mechanics. Drawing oxygen from water would become easy. He could read minds, and another talent presented itself that would filter out the terrifying static and interference of another person's thoughts, allowing him to home in on one specific idea. It was chilling and thrilling, but he passed it by.

Amazing, but none of this was of use to him.

The great red star of contagion throbbed and glowed right across his universe, pregnant with possibility.

He searched for anything that might help, skimming from one star to the next, understanding the amazing gifts they might grant him but knowing that none of them would be of use. In his desperation he moved faster, and soon his mind was aflood with new talents he had yet to use. Some of them he did not truly understand, because they were more obtuse. Beyond the normal bounds of human behaviour. *Maybe I could talk with the monsters*, he thought, but even that would not be of use. Not for what he needed.

Talk could not consume nuclear fire. A mind sensitive to thoughts or heat, movement or deviousness, could not cast aside the sun-hot flash that would soon bloom across London. Angry and scared, Jack opened his eyes and burst from his inner world. He found that he'd been panting hard and sweating, and Lucy-Anne was kneeling beside him looking concerned. He took the bottle of water she offered and drank deep, seeing stars.

"It's hopeless, isn't it?" she asked.

Jack did not answer. He looked at Fleeter, waiting to catch her eye. When she looked at him at last, he spoke.

"You and me," he said. "We're the only hope."

Fleeter shook her head. "I don't think so."

"Yes!" he said. "We flip, go to the bomb. Move it somehow. Carry it, drag it, whatever. Get it on a boat, sail out into the North Sea. We've got time. Eight hours here is eight days for us, or more."

She shook her head slowly, mouthing, *No.*

"Fleeter . . ." he said, and he wondered what her real name might be.

"You've never been flipped for more than a few seconds real-time," she said. "I have. I know what it feels like, what it does. It feels like *forever*. After the first few minutes you find it hard to function. Your body shuts down. A distance grows, and it's harder and harder to move or get back. It's a transitory thing, Jack. Like jumping around while everyone blinks. It's a trick, and I don't think we can trick time, or nature, or whatever it is that much."

"Don't think, or don't know?"

"Damn it, Jack, I know you're desperate, but don't blame me that it won't work!" Fleeter seemed serious, her usual smile absent. "Besides, you know what happens when we move things when we're flipped. Everything's speeded up in this world. We move the bomb, nudge it, drop the bloody thing, and who knows what'll happen?"

"So it's a long shot," Jack said.

"The longest."

"It probably won't work."

"No. It won't work."

Jack nodded and took another drink of water. "If you won't help me, I'll do it myself." He climbed to his feet and ran his fingers through his sweat-damped hair.

"Jack, no," Lucy-Anne said. "I'll not lose you as well."

"Then dream me safe," he said, smiling. He hugged Lucy-Anne, and as she hugged him back, she stiffened.

"What?" Jack asked.

"Andrew," she said. "He's here."

"Jack!" Jenna called from the restaurant outside. "Everyone! Someone's here."

Lucy-Anne pulled away and rushed through the swing doors, and Rhali stirred at the raised voices.

"What's happening?" she asked.

"I think a ghost's come to visit," Jack said. Fleeter went first, then he helped Rhali to her feet and supported her through into the restaurant.

Just inside the front doorway stood someone who was barely there.

"Lucy-Anne," the ghost breathed, his voice barely a whisper. "I can stop the bomb. But I need your friends' help."

CHAPTER TEN SEVEN

"How did you find me again?" Lucy-Anne asked.

"How could I not?" The remnant of Andrew stood close to the restaurant window as if avoiding shadows. Sunlight barely touched him. She could see that he was trying to be his old self for her—the cheeky smile, the way he pretended to lean against the wall—but everything was subsumed beneath his ethereal sadness.

"What will happen to you?"

"I've already gone," Andrew said. "You have to accept that, and understand it. I'm only here as an echo."

"But you *are* real. If you weren't, how could you be helping us? How could you have helped this man you've hidden away?"

Andrew shrugged, and for a moment he really was his old self, so much so that Lucy-Anne laughed. "Weird times," he said.

"Yeah. Tell me about it."

The others were bustling. Andrew's appearance was a shock, but now they were filled with a new sense of urgency and purpose. Jack's frustration at not being able to help had been palpable, and his insistence that he would do alone what Fleeter said was impossible together had been a sign of his desperation. Now, there was another way.

Lucy-Anne only hoped the man was still where Andrew had left him.

"Come with us?" Lucy-Anne asked.

"I'll be watching you," he said.

"My guardian angel."

"I wish." Andrew lifted a weightless hand and moved it close to her face, but not close enough to touch. She guessed he did that for her; to not feel his presence might be too much. But she could see from his eyes that he also did it for himself.

Andrew could no longer feel, and much about his sister must remain a memory.

"I'm so sorry," she said. The tears came, quiet but forceful. Andrew watched, helpless, able only to soothe her with hushed words. He whispered of their parents and how proud they would be of Lucy-Anne for carrying on, and being strong. He sang a song they'd made up when they were both young, nonsense lyrics about a frog and a toad walking a long road. It made Lucy-Anne laugh, and cry some more. She felt far too young to suffer from painful nostalgia, but Doomsday had made everyone grow old. That was one of its unspoken effects—it had made everyone involved, and the country as a whole, age.

"Ready," Sparky said. He stood behind Lucy-Anne and placed his hand on her shoulder, and she closed her eyes and pretended the contact was from Andrew. When she turned around and opened her eyes, Sparky was staring wide-eyed at Andrew, his Adam's apple bobbing up and down. "Whoa," he said.

"Yeah," Lucy-Anne said. "And yes. Ready. All of us together."

Sparky leaned in and gave her a wet kiss on the cheek, and as she pushed him away she was surprised at the sound of her own laughter.

They were preparing to leave the restaurant, possessed of a newfound urgency. Even Rhali seemed more lively and alert, and Jack had to shove his guilt over her to the back of his mind. He should be supporting her, listening to her story and helping her overcome whatever had happened to her in the Choppers' custody. Instead, he was rushing her back across London.

But individual needs were meaningless in the face of the catastrophe hanging over them. Millions had already died in London, and for Jack that made any more needless deaths all the more painful.

Lucy-Anne stood close to the front of the restaurant where the ghost of her brother cast no shadow. Sparky and Jenna gathered whatever drinks they could find, and knives for weapons.

Fleeter paced. Losing her constant smile suited her, because Jack no longer felt mocked. But he could still not trust her. That could only come with time they didn't have.

And then Emily crossed Jack's mind, so vibrant and there that for a moment he looked around for her. Then he smiled and closed his eyes, and knew that he could reach out to her so easily. Perhaps that would help. Knowing where she and his mother were, sensing their safety . . . maybe all that would help him through what was to come.

He grasped the talent and a dizzying surge made him sway. He heard and sensed hurried movement and held up one hand.

"Okay, I'm okay," he said. "Give a minute. I just need a minute."

Emily became his centre, and he allowed himself to drift towards her. He saw beyond London. There was no longer a sense of movement, but his perception shifted over the shattered city, past the devastated Exclusion Zone, and across the heads of the military still encircling what was left. Fields and roads passed beneath him, and small, deserted communities that had been abandoned after Doomsday. Scale changed as he dipped down, skimming over the landscape, then rooftops, and then settling at last in the playground of an old country primary school.

Emily was there, along with his mother. His sister grinned and squealed his name, jumping up and rushing around the playground with her arms held up, trying to grab him. His mother smiled and looked up at the sky. *She believes, too*, Jack thought, but of course she did. Doomsday had made her something special—a healer—and she knew that he'd been touched by Nomad.

Jack, I did it! Emily said. *I spread the word, and the photos, and everything is changing.*

It is, his mother said. *London's story will change again very soon.*

At first Jack thought they were talking about the bomb. But there was no way they could know, and as his consciousness dipped closer to his mother, he saw her confident smile.

They're coming! Emily said. *Hundreds of them, maybe thousands. I did it just like you said, and—*

—a jolt as Jack saw what she'd done, relayed either from her own memory, or perhaps painted by whatever talent had taken hold of him.

Emily with the camera she'd retrieved on her way back out of London, through the tunnels, Fleeter guiding her and her mother, a brief flash of violence as Fleeter—

Emily and his mother, alone now, hurrying across countryside with the weight of London behind them. Lights speckle the landscape; farms, hamlets, places where normal people are living almost-normal lives so close to the toxic city. His family are glad to be out, but sad that Jack is not with them. Go to Cornwall, he'd told them, but he can see from the set of Emily's face that—

She has no intention of doing what he'd told her. Instead, they break into the school under cover of darkness, do their best to seal off a small office by covering the window with several layers of curtains, and fire up the computer. It's a decent laptop with a good Internet connection. Emily connects the camera and downloads the pictures she's taken, and the film clips, and then—

Their mother finds some food and drink, and sits back while Emily works. The love she exudes for her daughter is overwhelming. As is her sadness at the two years of her daughter's life she missed. Jack sees his mother's tears even though Emily does not, and that makes him wonder—

I'm ready, Emily says, sitting back and stretching her stiff limbs. *Don't hesitate*, their mother says. *I wasn't. I was just enjoying the moment. I wish Jack could be here to see this*. She presses return and—

She has learned so much. Jack never knew she'd been watching him so closely, and Jenna when she worked on their computer in their buried camp in the woods—Camp Truth they'd called it, and now everything Emily had learnt there would be put to the test, the real truth its burden. Emails are sent in small blocks to avoid spam filters, attachments encrypted, any text bland and inconspicuous. Twenty, sixty, a hundred, worming their way through wires and across the ether, and while within the first second a large percentage are intercepted, examined, catalogued, flagged for inspection, and locked away in secure servers across the southeast, a few get through and find their intended recipients. Then the true dispersal begins. Sleeping computers wake, dormant servers fire up, and automated email accounts start forwarding emails to millions of addresses across the country. Most are caught and deleted by provider spam programmes, many more are attacked by security code written to look for precisely these messages—images scanned, tones and colours and content analysed by algorithms so complex that they require terabytes of power. From every million emails sent, perhaps a hundred land in inboxes, and of these maybe thirty are opened. From there, it is out of the virtual hands of the web and into the consciousness of human beings.

While emails fly and die, further messages are sent to the computer in Camp Truth. They'd christened it Marty so they could talk about it in company, and Jenna had treated it like another friend. Alone, it beeps and buzzes as its fan whirrs up, and the screen comes to life to illuminate the place where so many of their hopes had been kept alive. Jack senses the scene, and whilst exciting, it is also sad. The people who had been there mere days ago have all changed now, and discovering the fates of their various family members means they will never be the same again.

Jenna's programmes, worked on so diligently for months, start working. Images are dispersed to scores of websites, and to hundreds of people hiding online under a web of aliases and false provider information. Photographs and films taken within London soon pop up all across the Internet. Reaction is swift—the authorities' preparedness for such an eventuality shocks Jack, even though he has seen evidence of it so many times before—and websites crash like a series of virtual dominoes. But the spread of information is now speedier than any attempt to suppress it. And while ten websites crash, one will always survive to pass on information.

A film of the Exclusion Zone, with Jack and Lucy-Anne staring around in shock . . .

Jack's mother in the Underground station, and behind her the beds taken with dead and dying . . .

Choppers cruising the streets in their blue vehicles . . .

Nomad, mysterious, ethereal, with the sad, empty city behind her . . .

More images that betray the truth that has been kept from the world. Film clips that show the incredible things that have happened within London, and display that it is not a dead, toxic place as the world has been told.

Jack saw the truth spreading across Britain like blood finding its way through an organism's arteries and veins.

And as he finally drew back towards his universe of potential, he used Rhali's gift to sense the mass of people moving quickly towards London. Roads were heavy with vehicles. Their gravity was huge. And they were all coming to find people they had lost.

"Bloody hell, mate, I thought you were gone!" Sparky was kneeling next to him, Jenna and Lucy-Anne behind him.

"I was," Jack said. "I reached out to Emily. Saw what she's done. And . . ." He actually laughed out loud, and it felt so good. "And she's a genius! She's contacted Marty. She and my mum didn't get the hell away like I told them to, but are holed up in a school maybe twenty miles outside the Exclusion Zone. She used everything on the camera."

"And it was all stopped by the Choppers," Jenna said. "Go on. Tell me that. And they'll have triangulated on Camp Truth, too."

"No," Jack said, smiling. "A lot got through. The word's out. We've done what we always wanted to do, and now there are people coming towards London. Loved ones, those who always half-believed like us, they're all coming here to see what's left."

"And they're being stopped?" Sparky said.

"I'm not sure," Jack replied.

"Bloody hope they are."

"All the more reason to follow Andrew straight away," Lucy-Anne said. "What if they break through?"

"What do you mean?" Jenna asked.

"The truth got out there are just the wrong time," Lucy-Anne said. "It's what we've always wanted, but if so many people know, they won't be able to stop them."

"The Choppers will stop them coming close, just like they always stopped anyone leaving," Fleeter said bitterly.

"Really?" Lucy-Anne asked. "How? With force?"

"No," Jack said. "No, they can't. Oh. Oh, shit. There'll be press, reporters, web journalists. They'll try to stop them, but they won't be able to use force. And if there are enough people, they'll just march on London. Everything's been blown wide open."

"And because of that, it's not just London in danger now," Rhali said.

"That bomb can't explode!" Jenna said.

"Right," Lucy-Anne agreed. "And so we follow Andrew."

Fleeter flipped out, her disappearance causing a *thud!* that cracked one of the restaurant's front windows.

For a moment Jack thought of following. But even seconds might count now, and he would no longer desert his friends.

"Come on," he said. Without another word they left the restaurant and followed a ghost along London's haunted streets.

Walking behind Andrew was like living a memory.

Lucy-Anne and Andrew had never actually walked the streets of London together. She understood now that it was a proximity thing—people travelled from all over the world to visit London, but when you lived almost in its back garden, the need to visit receded. Her parents had been many times, and she and Andrew had visited separately, both with their respective schools and their parents. But they had never enjoyed these sights together.

Neither did they enjoy them now.

She had to keep reminding herself that this was not really Andrew before her. It was an echo of him, a dream remnant, and his true self was gone to dust on Hampstead Heath. Nomad had lied to her about not finding him, but she understood why. Andrew had not wished to give her hope.

Yet when her own chances had become hopeless, he had come.

Andrew led them along the north bank of the Thames, and at Vauxhall Bridge they crossed and headed northeast. Lucy-Anne wondered if she was in a dream, and realised that much of her time since entering London had felt like that. Sometimes she knew, and sometimes she did not. Sometimes she thought she knew, but then something would happen that would confuse her, send her concept of what was real and what was dreamlike spinning.

It was her friends who connected her to reality now. She was aware of them close behind her, all of them so pleased to see her again, their love for her uncomplicated by London and what it had become. With the city about to be turned into an atomic wasteland, she felt safer with them than anywhere else.

"How far?" she asked.

Andrew answered, "Maybe a mile," and Lucy-Anne was not sure whether he'd spoken the words or answered in her mind.

Gunfire crackled in the distance. They all dropped, huddling against a timber builders' hoarding. Lucy-Anne looked back at Jack. He was frowning, and there was something about his eyes that scared her. They looked empty. More vacant than Andrew's, less human than some of those creatures' eyes she had seen in the north.

"Reaper," Jack said. "He and his Superiors are hunting."

More gunfire, and then they heard the strained sound of a helicopter in trouble. About a mile to the east the aircraft rose above rooftops, spinning slowly as if piloted by someone unused to the controls. As it levelled at last and dipped its nose to power away, something struck it from the sky. The blast wave was not visible, but the helicopter's rotors were stripped away and flung behind it, its shell deformed, and it dropped quickly. In seconds it had disappeared from view, and a dull crump was followed moments later by a slowly expanding smudge of smoke.

"If Fleeter did go to him, maybe he didn't bother listening," Sparky said. None of them had suggested that she'd gone back to the Superiors, but they'd all been thinking it.

"Or maybe he's just having some fun on the way here," Jenna said.

"We just saw people die!" Rhali said.

"We've seen a lot of people die," Jenna said, not unkindly. "Come on. I don't want to stay on the streets. It's spooky, like someone's watching me."

"That'll be me," Sparky said. "Watching your arse."

Andrew had been motionless throughout the exchange, and he headed off again without a word or a glance at Lucy-Anne. *I'll be with him*, she thought. *When my time comes I'll be with him, because I'll dream myself to never die.* But she was not sure his was any sort of existence. She'd never believed in God or an afterlife, but surely true death would be preferable to whatever he had now.

They weaved through the streets, past traffic stalled for two years, seeing evidence here and there of more recent activity, and all the while the weight of Lucy-Anne's gift—or curse, she had yet to decide—pressed upon her.

She remembered those dreams she'd had of Nomad. The first was close to the London Eye, seeing Nomad and then the flash of the explosion silvering the scene, heat singeing trees to stark black sculptures and stripping her flesh away, while Nomad turned and smiled, untouched. And another dream of meeting her in the park and the same flash, the same skeletal outcome.

Reliving them now, Lucy-Anne tried to change them. Nomad turns to smile at her, and the explosion does not come. Instead, Lucy-Anne invites her to sit and talk, and they discuss Rook and what might have been.

Lucy-Anne caught Jack looking at her strangely, and she realised she was smiling. But changing her memory of dreams was nothing like changing the dreams themselves. It felt random and ineffectual, whereas lucidly altering her own dreams felt . . . godlike.

"What?" Jack asked.

"Just thinking," she said.

"What about?"

"The future."

They walked on in silence, and she knew that they'd all heard the brief exchange. She wondered what they were thinking right then, of a future that seemed so short.

CHAPTER ELEVEN SIX

"Six hours," Jack said. "We'd better hope this is all true." It had not escaped him that they had put their futures in the hands of a ghost. And that they were following him, or it, to where he said the saviour of that future now hid.

"Yeah," Sparky said. "We'd be hard pushed to get to a safe distance now, anyway."

"Jack could," Jenna said. There was no accusation in her voice at all, but Jack knew exactly what she was insinuating: that he could pass on a power to help them all escape.

And he was still fighting with that. He wasn't sure exactly what delving into that bright red star of potential would do. He was fairly certain that he could bestow powers, though he was not sure how he could choose which ones to give, nor the control he'd have over them. But he also thought it likely that he would pass on the contagion itself, just as Nomad had to him. Even thinking about it planted the taste of her finger on his tongue. In him, the threat of contagion was a bright red promise, yet it was contained. If two people possessed it, that containment was no longer assured. And if he passed it on to all of his friends . . .

That red star could change the world, and Jack did not feel that he had any right to do so.

But would he let his friends die? If it came down to it and they were an hour away from the explosion, would he not touch them all, give them Fleeter's power, and flee from London with them?

He wasn't at all sure. He saw the way Lucy-Anne looked at Andrew's wraith, and knew that there were some things worse than death. And if all went well, he would not even be faced with such a decision.

"We're close," Andrew said.

"Look," Rhali said. She had been silent since crossing the river, almost ghostlike herself. Now she pointed along the road, and only then did Jack see the movement. Perhaps Rhali had sensed it for some time.

A group of three strange people were passing across the street, emerging from a narrow side-road and clambering over stalled cars. Creatures from the north.

They ducked down low.

"Rhali?" Jack whispered.

"They're heading for the museum," she said. "There are many more there already, and even more still travelling." She frowned, her thin face pinched. "And there's something else."

"*What* else?" Sparky asked.

"Choppers," Rhali said. "At least, I think they're Choppers. They're moving as I'm used to seeing them moving."

"And how's that?" Jack asked.

"Quickly."

"Could be more of them," Jenna said, nodding towards the shapes. A man loped like a wolf. A woman seemed to flow across the road, trailing gossamer limbs that barely touched the ground.

"So where's this man?" Jack asked. No one answered, no one moved. "Andrew!"

The wraith turned its head, and Andrew's ghost seemed to be dreaming.

"I said where's the man who can stop all this?"

"His name's Hayden," Andrew said, pointing along the road at a multi-storey car park. "And I left him there, hiding."

"Let's hope he listened to you," Jack said. "If he tried to move on alone, he'll probably be dead."

As it turned out, he had not listened.

They climbed the concrete staircase, and Andrew showed them the Range Rover where he'd told the man to wait. It was empty, doors open. There were no signs of violence, but neither was there any sign of Hayden. Wherever he'd gone, and why, he had left them no message.

"Shit!" Sparky said. "So now what?"

"Now we look for him," Jack said.

"Something spooked him," Sparky said. "This place sure as shit spooks me."

Jack nodded in agreement. The car park was half-filled with cars, all of them left here two years ago by people who'd all expected to return.

"So where would he have run if he was spooked?" Jenna asked.

"Up," Jack said. "Further away from the street."

"My thoughts exactly," Sparky said. He slapped Jenna's butt and ran back towards the staircase door.

"We'll take the other staircase!" Jack called after him, and Sparky waved over his shoulder. Jenna followed him. She looked scared as she smiled at Jack, and he knew why, because he felt it himself. *I don't like us being split up. Not this close to the end, whatever that end might be.* He watched the door swing closed then led the way up a ramp towards the car park's opposite corner. He didn't want to miss Hayden by letting him slip down one staircase while they climbed another.

The car park was built on a series of split levels with wide up and down ramps at either end. Jack had been in scores of places like this with his parents, and as a kid he'd loved them, and had even had a model car park at home in which he stored his large collection of toy cars. He didn't love this one. The parked cars were testament to lives ruined or lost, and now it had become a vertical maze in which their one last hope might be hiding.

But what if he isn't? he thought. *What if he fled an hour ago and is out there in the streets?* Jack tried to shake the idea, but his imagination was running riot. Even though he hadn't yet met Hayden, he saw him being chased along streets by misshapen people, their teeth bared, hunger giving them energy and pace. They would catch him and rip him apart. And somewhere in the mess of brain matter spattered across the dry gutter would die the memory of how to stop the bomb.

"Hurry!" he said to Rhali and Lucy-Anne. "Come on, we've got to hurry!" He barged through the door into the stairwell and started up, and then came to a sudden standstill. Rhali bumped into him.

"What?" she said, startled.

"The ramps," Jack said. "Stupid of me! He could easily just slip down the car ramps while we're trying to find him."

"I'll stay," Rhali said. "I'll wait on this level, and if I see him I'll shout as loud as I can."

"But what if—?" Jack began.

"I don't think he's a threat," Andrew said. His voice was chilling. "He only wants to do what you want to do and stop the bomb."

Jack didn't like any of this, but could only nod in agreement. He watched Rhali walking back between the parked cars as the door swung closed, and he couldn't help thinking that he would never see her again.

"This is so screwed," Lucy-Anne said.

"Yeah. Tell me about it. Come on."

Jack took the steps three at a time. Another staircase, another building, and he expected at any moment to be shot at or attacked, because it seemed that's what his life had been since entering London. Nomad's touch throbbed within him, manifested as that amazing, terrible red star, and it had made him the centre of things. None of them had wanted any of that. All of this had been forced upon them, and he felt a sudden rush of intense love and respect for his friends and the way they were handling everything. They could have walked away, but none of them had.

None of them would.

Four storeys, eight flights of stairs, and the stench of the stairwell brought an uncomfortable flash of familiarity—it stank of piss. Every car park staircase he'd ever been in seemed to smell the same, and for a disconcerting moment, before they emerged onto the car park's open upper level, Jack thought perhaps everything was back to normal.

Then they emerged onto daylight, and awful reality came to the fore once more.

Two creatures from the north were attacking a car. They looked almost human apart from their limbs, which were black and shiny like a beetle's. They were using them to score metal and pummel glass, and it looked as if they had been there for a while. The car was a mess. Jack thought they'd be inside within minutes, and whoever they were seeking would be finished.

"Hey!" Sparky called from across the car park, emerging from the stairwell on the other side. "Hey, uglies!"

"No, Sparky!" Jack shouted.

The creatures both jumped on the car and watched, back to back, limbs raised in front of them in a defensive gesture.

"Hayden," Andrew said, and Jack had already seen the pale face at the car's rear window.

Jack ran. Sparky's shout had been brave but foolhardy; if they went after Sparky, he and Jenna had nothing to protect themselves with. This was all up to Jack.

He delved deep as he ran, but he already knew that these things were beyond his ken. They had evolved physically, a painful, shattering change that had left most of them half-mad from the continuing agonies, and raging. Even if he could find and touch the ability to do the same, he would not. He thought perhaps that darkest part of his universe—beyond the stars, way out past everything he knew and many talents he did not yet know—was the infinity of their pain, and he had no wish to go there at all.

But perhaps he could communicate with them. Along with their monstrousness came a high level of intelligence, and if he could appeal to that, maybe this would not have to end in more violence and death.

He paused a few steps from the car and nodded at Hayden, trying to communicate a sense of calm. The man looked terrified, and Jack could not blame him. The things resembled humans in form, but the resemblance stopped there. Their eyes were dark and shiny. Faces were slick, skin smooth and featureless. They exuded no personality, and looking at them was distinctly unsettling. But Jack did his best not to look away.

"The man in the car is precious," Jack said. "He can stop something terrible from happening. You might know about the bomb, you might not. But I want him alive and safe. And I don't want to have to fight you for him."

One of the creatures hissed, the other raised its heavily clawed arms, and Jack turned his head and shouted, channelling the talent he had already used so devastatingly. He put a lot into it—this was no time for a subtle demonstration—and he felt power thrumming through him, setting him on fire. He liked it. But he berated himself, because relishing it was what had turned Reaper bad.

The reinforced concrete wall, topped with a heavy metal railing, shattered out into space, and four cars were forced out after the shattered rubble, bodies crunched, windows shattering, wheels screeching across the concrete floor. They tumbled from view and then impacted the ground below several seconds later. Even before the two creatures had recovered from their shock, Jack had moved closer to them. He was almost in touching distance.

They looked at him with wide eyes.

"Move away from the car," he said. He was shaking with the remnants of the tremendous power, and he had to breathe deeply to cast it down.

One of the creatures laughed.

"Jack!" Rhali's voice, and it was coming closer.

The creatures scampered from the car and clattered away, but not too far. They slipped behind a big BMW and peered out at Jack, and he couldn't shake the conviction that they were waiting for something.

"Jack!" Rhali burst from the stairway into the open air, panting, sweating, looking as if she was about to collapse. "Jack, there are things coming!"

"What things?"

"I don't know, they're like people but . . ." She saw the two creatures watching. They'd become braver now, and they emerged from behind the BMW and scratched threateningly at the vehicle's paintwork. "Yeah. Like that."

"Jack can waste them all!" Sparky shouted. He and Jenna drew close, and though danger was also approaching, Jack felt better that they were all together once more. Even Andrew was still there, close to the car. Lucy-Anne had helped the man open the distorted door, and he was standing slowly, utterly terrified. Jack thought perhaps he'd been driven mad.

"You can do this?" Jack asked.

"Wh . . . what?"

"Hayden. That's your name, right?"

He nodded.

"So Hayden, you can stop the bomb if we get you to it?"

Hayden half-nodded, shrugging at the same time.

"Don't do that!" Jack shouted. "Don't give me any doubts! I might have to kill people, now. These things, they're still people. Just as much as the poor sods you bastards have been cutting up are people."

"I haven't cut any—"

"So tell me you can stop the bomb!"

Hayden nodded. "Given time."

"How much time?" Jack asked.

"I'll need an hour with the bomb. And peace and quiet. And the right tools."

"And how would you like your fucking steak cooked?" Sparky asked.

Jack laughed, high and loud, and felt his own sense of control wavering. He almost puked.

"Everyone in that one," Sparky said, nodding at a Mazda estate car.

"Plan?" Jack asked.

"If there's any battery left I can hot-wire it, and it's down to them to get out of the way." He slapped Jack's shoulder, and the gesture proved he knew so much about his friend.

"Good plan," Jack said. "And if everything goes wrong . . ."

"Then we've got you," Sparky said. "Superman. Our secret weapon. Hulk, smash!"

"I'll smash you in a minute. Get the bloody car started!"

Sparky saluted, grinned, and they all ran to the car. The door was open. The wheels weren't completely deflated. And there wasn't even a mummified corpse in the driver's seat.

Bonus! Jack thought. *Maybe things are turning our way.*

Then he froze as, on the next level down, he heard the sharp, rapid scraping of chitinous limbs.

Andrew drifted away, and when Lucy-Anne started after him Jack held her arm.

"I don't think they can hurt him," he said. Andrew glanced back and seemed to nod, and then he passed between two parked cars and disappeared from view.

"Come on, come on!" Sparky said. He'd opened his pocket knife and forced the covering beneath the steering column, and now he was hunkered down, bent almost double in the driver's seat as he spread a knot of wires, stripped some, then sat back. "Send a prayer to the god of car thieves," he said, and he touched two wires.

The engine growled . . . and then wound down with a tired yawn.

"Battery's flat!" Jenna said.

"You. In the car." Sparky grabbed Jenna and shoved her towards the driver's seat. Jack winced even before Jenna shoved back against her boyfriend—she wouldn't be told anything.

"Don't you treat me like a—"

"We push, you bump start the car!" Sparky said, exasperated. He looked across the split level, down at where those creatures were now sprinting for the ramp up to their level. "Maybe thirty seconds. Go! Second gear, clutch down, lift the clutch when I say, the car'll jerk a bit, then when it bites ease on the gas. But don't go without us."

"Rhali and Hayden, in the back," Jack said. "Keep the doors open for us."

Jack, Sparky and Lucy-Anne went to the back of the car and started pushing. They strained and groaned, propping their feet against the wall behind them and pushing harder, and then Sparky shouted, "Take the bastard hand brake off!" Jenna did so, and with a squeal of frozen brakes the car eased forward.

"Now," Sparky said, "push as hard and fast as you can."

They pushed. The car rolled. Jack glanced up and saw Rhali's concerned face watching them through the back window, and he tried to smile. Then through the car and out the front windscreen he saw the movement of things reaching the top parking level.

"They're here," he said.

"Then push harder! We need to get close to the ramp. That way if the engine doesn't start we can coast that far at least."

"And then?" Lucy-Anne said between them. But Sparky did not answer.

"They've stopped," Jack said, but he held no hope that the things would not attack. They merely seemed to be formulating a strategy. The two that had been trying to get Hayden were conversing with three others in a language Jack could not imagine, gestures and loud clicking sounds replacing the spoken word. They spread out, three stalking forward while two others scampered back down to the level they had just emerged from. They had seen what Jack could do, and were spreading themselves out as much as possible.

Even if Jack and his friends did manage to start the car, they would have a gauntlet to run.

They're just people! Jack thought, wishing he could communicate, reach out to them. But "just" held no meaning anymore.

"Now!" Sparky said.

Jenna eased up on the clutch. At first Jack felt a resistance, then the vehicle jerked forward and he almost stumbled to the ground. Sparky grabbed him, and Lucy-Anne was already darting for one open side door. The car jarred forward, the engine coughed and growled, Jack caught a faceful of foul air from the exhaust, and then Sparky shouted, "Gas!" Jenna pressed on the gas and the engine roared.

"Yes!" Jack punched the air and ran with Sparky. Jenna slammed on the brakes and dropped out of gear, revving the engine some more. Smoke hacked from the exhaust.

And the creatures were coming. One each on the left and right, leaping across the roofs of parked cars, and one straight for the car. Jack was sure he saw sparks kicked up from their nightmarish limbs.

"In!" Sparky shouted. "Jack!"

But Jack waited until his friends were safely inside, his breath held and a shout ready to be unleashed. He did not *want* to kill, but if he had to . . .

Sparky was in and Jack darted for the door. His strong friend grabbed his arms and pulled, and even as Jack sprawled across the others' laps in the back seat, Jenna gunned the gas and pulled away.

Hayden had climbed into the front seat and he cowered down, terrified. And his fear was good. If he'd been sitting up straight he might have died.

The creature must have leapt directly at the windscreen, jumping over the bonnet of the moving vehicle and using its two arms as spears. The windscreen starred opaque, Jenna screamed, but she did not slow down. Sharp insectile limbs slashed across Hayden's seat and shredded the headrest. The glass shattered and fell inwards in a shower of diamond shards, and Jenna punched the windscreen in front of her, clearing her view and spinning the steering wheel at the last moment. The Mazda's bumper scraped across a wall as the car slewed to the right, and the creature emitted an ear-splitting shriek as it was wrenched from the bonnet.

"Floor it!" Sparky shouted. Jenna pumped on the gas and the engine roared, and she spun the wheel again as they bumped onto the next level down.

Jack pulled himself into a sitting position between Sparky and Rhali, and Lucy-Anne was pressed against the door beside Rhali.

"Is he . . . ?" she asked.

Jack leaned forward to look over the seats, terrified of what he might see. But Hayden stared up at him with wide eyes.

"He's OK. Jenna, you need to change gear."

"What?"

"You need to—"

"I haven't got a clue how to drive so just shut up and let me get on with it."

"Ease on the gas, foot on the clutch, slip into—" Sparky began.

"Shut the hell up!" she shouted. Remaining in second gear she drifted them wide into the ramp to the next level, rebounding from the wall again with a sickening crunch and a laboured screech of tearing metal.

"It's okay," Sparky said. "We don't need the bumper. Bumpers are overrated."

"Where the hell *are* those things?" Lucy-Anne asked. Jack twisted in his seat and looked behind at the shapes loping after them.

"Not finished yet," he said.

"Mate, can't you do anything?" Sparky asked.

"If I need to," Jack said. "But—"

It must have been on the car roof. Sitting there, planning, scheming, trying to figure out how best to get at the food inside. And the best way was to put their best defence out of action. Jack saw a flurry of movement, heard the dull whisper of strengthened glass breaking into countless pieces, and felt Sparky lean into him as he cringed away from the thrashing limb that swung into the car.

Then the impact across his face, and no more.

Blood splashed across Lucy-Anne's face. It was a sickening warmth that quickly faded to cool, and she knew that Jack was dead.

Rhali screamed. Jack slumped to the side and rested against her, bleeding on her, and she started hyperventilating, trying to shove him away and hold his face at the same time.

"Jesus Christ!" Jenna shouted, because she'd seen everything in the rearview mirror.

"Drive!" Lucy-Anne shouted. She could taste Jack's blood when she opened her mouth. "Just fucking drive, Jenna!" If they stopped now—if they let those things get into the car—Jack was no longer here to do anything to help them.

Jack was no longer here . . .

She couldn't dwell on that, and neither could she check him out to make sure. Sparky was struggling and he needed her help, and really, everything might depend on her. Everything. Because Hayden was crying and gibbering in the front seat, and Rhali could only look at the bloody mess that had been Jack's face.

Not yet, not yet, Lucy-Anne thought. *I'll look in a minute. I'll try to find my best friend's pulse in a minute.*

Sparky had grasped the thing's limbs and was holding it up against the ceiling, pushing with all his might. It was dark and shiny like a beetle's carapace, ending in a sharp pincer-like arrangement that was even now shredding Sparky's shirtsleeve and the car's fabric ceiling. The thing was scrabbling up on the roof trying to maintain its purchase, and as Jenna swung them down another ramp and bounced from another wall, the limbs shifted position as the creature slid.

Lucy-Anne leaned across Rhali and Jack and thrust her hand into Sparky's jeans pocket. She worked her fingers against the folds and creases and found the knife, tugging it out, ripping the material, opening the blade, and without even looking at Sparky she leaned further over him and started slashing at the limb where it entered the window. Shoulder or elbow she couldn't quite figure out, but the thing squealed in agony as black blood spattered down across her forearm.

"Sparky!" she shouted. He heaved the limb back towards the window and then let go. The creature slid from the roof and bounced from the boot, squirming and thrashing when it struck the ground.

"Floor it!" Lucy-Anne screamed. She sat back against the door with the knife still in her hand, and realised that the thing's blood stank.

"Jack?" Jenna asked.

"Get us out of here or we'll *all* be dead!"

"Dead?" Rhali said. She spoke softly, but even above the car's labouring engine they all heard. It was a word that broke through such noise.

Lucy-Anne looked at Jack again, nervous, her heart fluttering. His face was a bloody mess.

"Just drive," she said.

Jenna seemed to become more confident. Though she did not attempt to change gear, and the engine screamed as she floored the gas between floors, she took the ramps more successfully, avoiding any more jarring impacts with the walls. On the third floor one of the tyres blew out and the car slewed sideways, but Jenna fought with the wheel and straightened them again. On the second floor she crashed into a Ford that protruded from the parking bays. The impact almost stalled the Mazda, but she slammed her foot on the gas, wheels screaming, the stench of burning rubber accompanying them as the Ford was shoved sideways and their car scraped past.

"Where are they?" Sparky said. He was looking behind them, ahead, and leaning cautiously sideways to peer from the shattered side window.

"Given up the chase?" Lucy-Anne asked.

"Maybe," he said. But they all remained on edge as they drove out from the shadowed car park into daylight.

"Too noisy," Lucy-Anne said. "Let's get a street away then dump the car."

"And we'll have to see to Jack," Sparky said. He was taking his first good look at his friend, and Lucy-Anne could see his fear.

"How is he?" Jenna asked. She kept glancing in the mirror. The car engine screamed in second gear. Hayden gibbered in the front seat.

Rhali stroked Jack's brow, and his face bled.

Her illness washing through her, Nomad raised her head and looked around. The tank was static and terrible. The wires and fail-safes glowed menacingly all around the display hall. All was silent.

"Jack," she said. She gasped, because something had changed. But whatever the change, Jack had made his choice.

And there was always Lucy-Anne.

CHAPTER TWELVE FIVE

In darkness and nothing, Jack thought he was with the monsters.

He had an awareness of who he was but not why he was here. He wanted to call his friends, but could not remember their names. He floated, or sank, or rose through darkness so complete that it had form and solidity. It was like swimming in black water, but here he could breathe.

The taste on his tongue was blood.

After an unknown time he started to make out a glow in the distance. At first it was a smudge on the night, a sheen in the blackness. He moved towards it, out of the stark nothingness where there were monsters, and it started to take on form. Countless points of light manifested, like sprinkles of salt on a black sheet the size of a field. The closer he approached, the clearer the image became, and the larger and more malevolent the deep blackness behind him.

That's my universe. His words were comforting. And as he thought them, the spread of light expanded rapidly until it filled his field of vision and he was inside it, enveloped and part of the light himself, and the blackness was banished to the distance.

Yet he still did not feel safe. He passed through this place that was his, and just off-centre was a warm red glow. It should have been inviting but was not. The warmth should have made him feel safe, but the opposite was true.

The glow was contagion. But it was not his to give.

"And it wasn't Nomad's to give either," he said. His voice was so loud that the stars shimmered, and somewhere beyond he felt a reaction to what he had said. *My friends heard me. They fear for me. But I have to make sure.* He moved closer to the throbbing red glow and saw that it was a star on its own, but one that contained universes. Impossible, incredible, terrifying universes that he could pass on with a touch, just as Nomad had passed this on to him.

None of this was natural. None of it should exist. His universe was a falsehood made real by a mad woman, and humanity could not endure it.

I'll always keep it to myself. Always. No matter what.

"Is he dead?"

Hayden had been the last to climb from the car and follow them, but now he was the first to speak.

"No, he's not bloody dead!" Sparky said. "And thanks would be welcome right now."

"Thanks?"

"For rescuing you?" Lucy-Anne said. She hated Hayden already and she hadn't even told him her name.

"Oh, right. Thanks."

Jenna had parked close to the front of an old discount furniture store, and carrying Jack between them they'd entered and moved quickly through to the back entrance. Lucy-Anne had pulled aside a pile of damp, rotting mattresses to reveal a fire escape, and she'd opened it with a kick. Sparky had then slung Jack over his shoulder and followed Lucy-Anne outside, passing across a small courtyard and along a narrow alley before emerging onto the next street. There, an abandoned Starbucks had become their hiding place. If those things had been pursuing them, they hoped that they'd now shaken them off. But if they did still follow, there was little they could do.

None of them would leave Jack behind, and Lucy-Anne was shocked at how vulnerable she now felt. Without realising it she'd quickly come to rely on Jack to protect them all.

"See if you can find any water," Jenna told Rhali. "Lucy-Anne, tissues or napkins, anything clean to mop away the blood."

"Me?" Sparky asked.

"Best keep watch," she said. Lucy-Anne caught the glance between her two friends; they knew how defenceless they all were now.

She climbed behind the counter and looked for napkins. The place had been ransacked at some point, but a drift of napkins remained on one of the lower shelves. Rhali found some bottled water, and Jenna went about cleaning Jack's wounds.

"I think it looks worse than it is," Jenna said.

"You shitting me?" Lucy-Anne said. "His eye's out, Jenna!"

"No. Eyelid's slashed, and that makes it look like his eyeball's damaged. But I don't think it is." She mopped blood, and Jack's eyes rolled.

There were other cuts all across the right side of his face, from his jaw up into his hairline. Jenna cleaned them with bottled water, but that thing that had attacked him, its horrid pincers . . . Lucy-Anne didn't like to wonder what germs it carried. She watched Jenna dab at the cuts, and then examine the deep bruise already forming across Jack's temple and into his hairline.

"That?" Lucy-Anne asked.

"Fractured skull," Hayden said. In a flurry of movement Sparky was up and at him, a seventeen-year-old boy pushing this thirty-year-old man back against the wall, forearm pressing against his throat, other hand fisted and drawn back ready to punch.

Hayden looked terrified.

"You haven't earned the right to say a single word about my friend," Sparky said. He released Hayden as quickly as he'd pushed him, turning back to Jack and squatting beside him. He leaned in close and examined the wounds that Jenna was tending. "So is it fractured?"

"I don't know," Jenna said. "I . . . I don't really know what I'm doing, Sparky. I can dab the blood away. Given the right kit I might even be able to patch his eye and bandage him up. But . . ."

She cleaned gently, lovingly. Jack shuddered.

"Come on, mate," Sparky said. He held Jack's hand and squeezed, moving his arm up and down, slowly so as not to shift him too suddenly.

"He's just knocked out," Rhali said. "That's all. The thing banged his head."

"It's really hard to be knocked out," Sparky said. "Not like in the movies. You have to do damage to knock someone out."

Oh no, oh no, Lucy-Anne thought. She had to lean against a table to prevent herself from slumping to the floor, biting her lip and drawing blood. She briefly considered letting herself drop into dreamland, dreaming Jack well again. But it might never last. And her wider fears included not only Jack.

She looked around at the others. Sparky and Jenna at least were thinking the same thing. They'd only known each other for two years, but they'd been through a lot, and she thought they were brothers and sisters. Family. The only family she had left, and she could not bear to mourn any more.

"We're wasting time," Lucy-Anne said. "You know that, don't you?"

None of them answered. Rhali looked up at her, about to speak, but she bit back the words. Hayden shuffled his feet. Jenna paused in her cleaning of Jack's wounds.

"We can't just leave him here."

"I'll stay," Rhali said.

"And it wasn't Nomad's to give either," Jack said, and they all held their breaths, ready for him to open his eyes. But he remained unconscious, shuddering occasionally. His skin was growing pale.

"Right," Sparky said. He stroked Jack's hand, eyes turning left and right as he thought something through. "Right. How long?"

"About five hours," Hayden said softly.

"Long enough," Sparky said. "You said you needed an hour."

"And peace and quiet. And the right tools."

"Tools," Sparky said. "Okay. You and me, we go and find the tools. We're close to the museum, so the others can rest here, and we go and find what you need."

Hayden seemed uncertain but he nodded.

"I'll come with you," Lucy-Anne said.

"Didn't for a moment expect you to stay sitting on your arse," Sparky said, grinning. He knelt beside Jenna. "Half an hour," he said. "Stay quiet."

She nodded.

"Stay safe!" Sparky said. He pulled her close and kissed her cheek roughly. "I love you." There was not a shred of embarrassment to his words.

"We're going to have to leave him," Lucy-Anne said as they emerged onto the street. Sparky held a hand up as he checked both ways, then waved them forward. They slipped from doorway to doorway, using parked cars and vans as cover.

"Yeah," Sparky said at last. "If he doesn't wake."

"Even if he does he'll be weak and have a monstrous headache," Lucy-Anne said.

"But it's Jack," Sparky said. "You know what he can do, how special he is. We need him. Don't you think? We'll need him to even get close to the museum, and here we are looking for bloody *tools*?"

"We have to do our best."

They never stopped walking. Sparky scanned their route, Hayden between them, and Lucy-Anne kept glancing behind them to make sure they weren't being followed. Or stalked. But she could sense a hopelessness in Sparky's movements. He was desperate, and that same desperation was manifesting in her.

She nudged Hayden. "See anything useful?"

"We need a hardware store," he said. "Maybe a repair shop. You know, washing machines, that sort of thing. A garage. Anywhere that might have a well-equipped toolbox."

"You were coming to defuse an atomic bomb without a toolbox?"

"The Superiors wiped out our vehicles," Hayden said. "Me and two others survived, ran, didn't have time to grab anything. We were lucky to get away with our lives, let alone any equipment."

"So where the hell are the other two?" Sparky asked.

"Spooky guy told me they were dead."

"You're risking your life when you could be running," Lucy-Anne said.

Hayden glanced back. "So are you."

"Okay," Sparky said. "Keep looking. Everything we've been through, I don't want to mess up now 'cos we didn't have a screwdriver."

"Let's cross over," Hayden said. "Take that side street. I spent some time around here couple of years before Doomsday. I think there's a locksmith's down there."

"That'd suit?" Lucy-Anne asked.

"That'd be perfect."

They crouched and crossed the street, pausing behind a van that had been turned onto its side. Listening. Watching for movement, and any signs of pursuit. There was a rattle of gunfire far in the distance, and Lucy-Anne glanced at Hayden. His eyes had gone wide and his head was to one side, listening.

"Your lot popping off a few more survivors?" Sparky asked.

Hayden did not rise to his bait. "No. Everyone's had the evacuation order, far as I know. That'll be something else."

"Yeah, guess who," Lucy-Anne said.

They turned a corner and moved along the new street, and five shops along was the locksmith's that Hayden remembered. The front door was open.

Sparky and Lucy-Anne waited close to the front of the shop while Hayden disappeared into the workshop at the back. As they kept watch they heard him rooting around for tools, dropping them into a metal box and mumbling to himself.

"Maybe we should just go," Lucy-Anne said. "Take him to the museum and leave Jenna, Jack and Rhali where they are. Pick them up on the way out, after it's done."

"No," Sparky said. "No way."

"But with Jack like that—"

"It's nothing to do with Jack," he said. "I want to be with Jenna, and I know she wants the same. When the end comes, you know?"

"But we're doing our best."

"Can't you feel it?" Sparky said. "The hopelessness of all this? Night's falling on London, Lucy-Anne. The end's close. Everything feels doomed, and what we're doing just feels so pointless. Clutching at straws."

"You've got to have hope."

"I do. I have hope that I can die with Jenna. With the girl I love.

And all of us together, too, when the time comes. We got more than we ever dreamed really, didn't we? Always wanted to expose the truth of what London had become, reveal the lie being told to everyone. And here we are in the middle of it all. I never thought . . ." He chuckled wryly, shook his head.

"That doesn't sound like the Sparky I know."

"Not sure I'm him anymore."

She wanted to rage, and cry. Instead, she pulled Sparky close and gave him a hard, quick kiss on the lips. Then she gripped his lapels.

"There's still hope," Lucy-Anne whispered. After everything, she was surprised that she was the one to say that. She thought of Nomad, and the explosion, and Rook falling and being killed even though she had dreamed him surviving. And the refrain repeated again and again in her mind as Sparky stared at her, unable to respond. *There's still hope . . .*

For a while Jack believed himself dead, because when he tried to rise from his star-speckled darkness he could not. Reality remained obscure and difficult to find. Like some people's idea of Heaven, it was beyond the universe he now knew.

But then he touched on a talent and plunged inside, and his perception changed. He floated in a blue sea that surrounded him on all sides and in all directions, and in places the sea was marred with frozen places, the ice a deep green colour, cracks seeping pain, sharp surfaces brushing against the sea and spreading more cold.

I know what this is, he thought, and he closed on one berg. The water grew colder and strong currents swirled through the sea, but he kept his course and reached out. The point between water and ice was ambiguous, but Jack felt power flowing through him and producing a warm, comforting heat. The berg began to melt. Green turned to blue.

He could make out more details about his surroundings, as if the gift of vision was becoming more defined, and he waited there until the berg was almost completely gone. At its centre remained a solid core, a scar on the blue ocean that would likely remain there forever.

But Jack knew that he had done enough, and he drifted away towards another spread of ice. This was much larger but less defined, like a sea of sludge within this endless ocean of blue. It was a deep purple colour, and shades and tones swirled and flowed in its depths. Jack paused for only a moment before allowing himself to enter. The floating sensation was different—more harsh edges, and the smell/taste was sickly and rich—and he exuded the healing warmth once again.

As the cold ocean around him faded from a rich purple to a comfortable blue, it began to take on more features. His senses burst alight. He could hear the mumble of voices, though as yet the words made little sense. He could feel contact against his skin—a pressure behind him from where he was lying down, and a repetitive caress against one extreme that might have been his hand. And he could smell coffee.

Coffee!

He tried talking, but the shades of purple still swallowed his words. More heat, more healing flow. What he was doing amazed him, though perhaps it should have come as no surprise. He possessed remarkable powers after all, and healing himself was not the most incredible thing he had ever done.

As the purple faded some more he cast his senses farther afield, and when he felt able, he tried to speak once more.

"Large latte, extra shot." Jack tried to sit up, and Jenna grabbed him beneath one arm, Rhali the other. When he was sitting he looked around at them all, saw the toolbox in Hayden's hand, nodded. "Good. Right. Let's go."

None of them spoke. There was a stiffness and soreness in Jack's right eye. It felt like someone had punched him there and it was swollen, but when he closed his left eye he could still see, though his vision was blurred.

And his head hurt like hell.

"But . . ." Lucy-Anne said.

"Mate," Sparky said.

"What?" Jack went to stand, but Jenna pressed her hand gently on his shoulder.

"For a moment we thought you were dead," she said. "Then it looked like your eye had been gouged out. And Hayden thought you had a fractured skull, and we weren't sure whether you'd even wake up or not. There was so much bleeding. You were shaking, and muttering things. And we just . . . didn't know."

"I'm fine," Jack said. "Bastard of a headache." He leaned into Rhali and she held him, kissing his forehead. He liked her breath against his face.

"You healed yourself," Sparky said. "How cool is that?"

"Doesn't feel like it's healed," Jack said. He lifted a hand to his face and touched his right eye, wincing when he felt the knotted flesh there, the hard scars that would probably remain forever.

"Dude, compared to what it was you're a supermodel," Jenna said, and they all laughed.

"So you got what you need?" Jack asked, nodding at the toolbox in Hayden's hand.

"Pretty much."

"Pretty much?" Sparky asked, and Hayden's eyes opened wider.

"Yeah, everything, got it all," he said.

"Right," Sparky said. "Heard some gunfire to the north, long way off. Other than that, things are quiet out there."

"That's what I'm afraid of," Jenna said. "Quiet things."

"Nothing close," Rhali said. "Nothing I can sense, anyway. That doesn't mean there aren't small groups of creatures out there. And the museum . . ." She closed her eyes again, swaying slightly. "Lots."

"How many?" Lucy-Anne asked.

Rhali shrugged. "Lots. And lots."

"Bridges to cross when we get there," Jack said. His rush of joy at surfacing to find his friends around him was quickly receding, and now the future only promised more pain, and trouble, and violence. And they didn't have very long left.

"What's the time?"

"Almost eight," Jenna said.

"Four hours."

Rhali helped him up and he smiled his thanks. He felt sick and weak, but he could not project that. They needed his strength. They needed to feel he still had their backs, and between blinks he saw that universe of talents he still had access to, and the red star of contagion he would never, ever touch.

"So what are we waiting for?" Jack asked.

Outside, the sun was touching the rooftops in the west.

CHAPTER THIRTEEN
FOUR

"What if you'd died?" Jenna asked him as they set off for the Imperial War Museum.

"No, Jenna."

"But if you *had*. We were desperate back there, Jack. And I was scared. I felt naked, exposed."

"There's no way I'd ever infect you. I'd never do that to anyone, you least of all."

"But it's a gift! The things you can do, Jack. The amazing things."

"I've killed people." Stating it like that, stark and plain, brought the reality home to Jack once again. Previously it had been a memory that haunted him, but now it was a truth that had been hauled into the fading sunlight and laid bare.

"They were trying to kill us." But Jenna spoke without conviction.

"I'll explain it when all this is over," Jack said.

"So we go closer to the museum," Jenna said. "Those things are there. Lots of them, according to Rhali. Some of them are like the others we met—more monsters than people. They're hungry. They attack us, we fight them off, you use some of your powers to smash them away or burn them or, I dunno, turn them into Muppets. But one gets through and kills you. You're dead, Jack. Deader than Miller with his brains blown out, and deader than Lucy-Anne's ghost brother. What happens then?"

"You do your best."

"But if I had your powers, we'd have insurance!"

"No, Jenna! They were never mine to own, and they're surely not mine to give."

He loved Jenna. She was a pure, kind, intelligent girl. Her desire for him to pass on his contagion was, he knew, largely for the reasons she had stated. But he was also aware of how his friends viewed him with a mixture of fear and awe, and there was an element of desire in Jenna's pleading as well. She wanted to be Wonder Woman to his Superman, and he supposed it was only natural.

"It's selfish, Jack," she said softly.

"No!" The others glanced back, but looked away again. Perhaps they could hear his conversation with Jenna, perhaps not. He didn't care. "It's the *opposite* of that. I have a weight on me that I can't shake off, ever. And if by some tiny miracle we do what we're trying to do and stop the explosion, and get out of London, what about me then? Have you thought about that?"

Jenna opened her mouth to speak, but then paused, and thought. Jack's normal life was over. He would be exposed—an oddity, a freak, someone to be examined or pointed at in the street—or he would living forever in hiding.

"And it's more than that," he said. "Too much to tell you. But no, Jenna, much as I love you and however much you ask, I can't curse you like that."

She did not respond. Jack was glad.

Andrew joined them again half a mile from the museum. He emerged from shadows and Lucy-Anne's heart fluttered, stealing her breath. Every time she saw him, grief hit home one more time.

"There are lots around the museum, and some inside," he said. "But they know they can't go inside. One tried, and the others killed her. There are traps everywhere, and the bomb's sealed in a tank. They're here to stop it, but they don't know how."

"We do," Lucy-Anne said. For the first time since his return, she saw a flicker of what might have been emotion cross his face. He seemed briefly happy, and she thought it was happiness for her. He wanted his sister to survive.

"But it's impossible to get close," Andrew said. He looked at Jack. "For all of you together, at least."

"Jack, maybe you could do what Fleeter does and carry Hayden inside," Lucy-Anne said.

Jack shook his head. "It's far too risky. When I carried Rhali out at Camp H we had a clear route, no distractions. And even then I hurt her. Here, I don't know the way, and there are dangers all over. One wrong move and I could kill him. And what about the booby traps?"

They all turned to look at Hayden. The Chopper looked at the friends, and they could all see in his expression that he felt excluded and alone. But he also understood that with these people—the kids who had grown up too fast, the boy with amazing powers, the ghost—lay his only hope.

"I didn't design the security, but I know the guys who did. They were briefed that once the bomb was armed and initiated, no one should be able to get close. So there are security measures, some linked to small explosive devices or toxic gas, a couple linked to Big Bindy itself."

"What sort of measures?" Jack asked.

"Trip wires."

"Easy," Sparky said. "We go slow."

"Infrared, air movement and body heat detectors, and lasers."

"Right. Not so easy."

"And some of them trigger the bomb?" Jack asked.

"Yeah, in case all the others fail or are breached. Open the tank it's planted in and it blows. And the trigger mechanism in the bomb is contained in a vacuum chamber—expose it to the air, it blows."

"Basically, fart anywhere south of the river and the bomb blows," Sparky said.

"I've been there," Andrew said. "Nomad is there also."

"Well if *she* can get in . . . !" Jenna said, staring pointedly at Jack.

"Maybe," he said. "Although she knows what powers she has, whereas I'm still feeling around for mine. Lots of trial and error. And besides, what good would it do if I *could* get in? A year ago I had trouble wiring a plug."

They heard a sound in the distance, a cross between a growl and a bark. It came from no dog Lucy-Anne had ever imagined.

"We should wait," she said. "Get off the road again and decide what we're going to do. As it is we're just marching towards the museum without a clue about what comes next. We need to come up with a plan."

"We don't have time," Jenna said.

"We'll only get one chance!" Lucy-Anne said. The cooling dusk air seemed to swirl about her as she spoke, as if in agreement. And then Fleeter stepped from the shadows and collapsed into the gutter.

"Shit!" Sparky said. "I wish she wouldn't do that."

Lucy-Anne was the first by her side, kneeling and reaching out for the strange girl. Even before she touched her she knew something was wrong.

"The sickness?" Jack asked. He sounded so childlike, so lost, that Lucy-Anne felt the burn of tears for her friend. But it was not the sickness.

"No," she said. "I think she's been shot."

"Close," Fleeter said. She held Lucy-Anne's proffered hand and squeezed. “Explosion. Got hit . . .” She swept her other hand across her left hip and down her thigh, not quite touching. There was plenty of blood, although much of it was dried and sticky.

“Who is this?” Hayden asked.

“A Superior,” Jack said. “She’s killed dozens like you.”

Lucy-Anne saw the look of terror on Hayden’s face and could not help smirking. *Really? Siding myself with Fleeter?* It was a strange thought.

They helped her up and guided her into a deep doorway.

“What happened?” Jack asked Fleeter. “Where did you go? Have you been outside London again?”

“Tried,” she said, wincing at the pain. As she spoke Jenna cut her blouse from hip to armpit, revealed the wounds, and started tending them.

“And?”

“Went with Reaper and the others,” Fleeter continued. “I didn’t know if he’d have me back. But Reaper . . . he’s special to me. I guess you knew that, Jack. And I’m sorry. He still cares for you, too. There are parts of him that are so strong and determined, and I always felt—”

“I don’t need telling what a bastard my father’s become,” Jack said. “You came back to us for a reason, so just tell us what happened.”

“We tried to get out,” she said. “Me, Reaper, Shade, Puppeteer, Scryer, a few others you’ve not seen or met. It was down to me and Shade to set some distractions.”

“We saw some of them,” Lucy-Anne said, remembering the plunging helicopter seen in the north.

“We went south,” Fleeter continued. She winced, Jenna apologised and continued cleaning her wounds. “I went ahead and scouted our route, and it seemed safe. Returned to Reaper and the others. We set off. But I must have set off an alarm of some sort. As we crossed the Exclusion Zone we hit a rapid deployment patrol."

"Nothing like that seems to have bothered Reaper in the past," Lucy-Anne said. "I saw him take down a helicopter with a shout."

"And I've seen him do so much more than that," Fleeter said.

"Not too bad," Jenna said, standing. "A few nasty cuts that should be stitched. No shrapnel in you that I can find.

Fleeter nodded her thanks.

"So what went wrong this time?" Jack asked.

"They had something," Fleeter said. "A gas, maybe. It was like . . ." She trailed off and looked at Jack. "You won't have felt it yet. The weakness. The sickness."

"We've seen enough of it," Lucy-Anne said.

"It seemed to boost the illness. I've felt it, and every time I flip I feel it more. But whatever they used on us made it all so much worse. And while we were down, they attacked."

"Who got away?" Jack asked, his voice flat. *He wants to know if his father is dead*, Lucy-Anne thought. And though Reaper was a beast, a killer, and no longer anything approaching a father to Jack and his sweet sister, she so hoped that he was still alive.

"Puppeteer was already dead when we came around," she said. "I think the illness was quite advanced in him, and whatever they used on us pushed him over the edge. We fought, but we were weakened. I flipped but couldn't move . . . I was as still as everything else around me. Reaper shouted, but knocked himself down. He became enraged. He has such pride, Jack, in what he can do, and suddenly losing control drove him mad."

"Madder," Sparky said.

"By then there were reinforcements coming in, on land and in the air. Choppers, scores of them, but they weren't shooting to kill.

They were trying to capture us. So we fought. They had Scryer, but she got free and ran. They shot her, then. I saw her go down, and she must have been hit by twenty bullets. Tore her apart. Shade disappeared and I haven't seen him since. Reaper retreated, and for a time he and I were together. We ran through the streets, and I could feel his fury and pain. Then I tripped and fell, hit my head, and when I came around I was on my own."

"He left you," Jack said.

"Perhaps he thought I was dead." She sounded so sad to Lucy-Anne, because she did not believe that at all.

"Sounds like they were taking their last chance to catch you," Jack said. "Maybe when this is over they still want subjects to experiment on. So they didn't follow you in to London?"

"No, I don't think so. I wandered for a while, then Reaper came to me again. He'd found Shade by then, and also Haru, the ice lady. And he told me what we had to do."

"Find us again," Jack said.

Fleeter nodded. She looked pale and alone, and Lucy-Anne almost felt sorry for her. "If the Superiors can't get out, what hope do we have?" Lucy-Anne asked.

"None," Sparky said.

"It doesn't matter," Rhali said. "We're out of time anyway. Fleeing London isn't our aim anymore." She pointed at Hayden. "It's all on him."

"Reaper's coming, Jack," Fleeter said. "Him, Shade, Haru. And me. We're all behind you, now. We've tried to fight. We've tried violence, and it didn't work. Stopping the bomb is the only way."

Jack did not respond. He was frowning, looking into a distance none of them could see, and perhaps seeing a future none of them *wanted* to see.

"I don't trust him at all," he said at last. "And I don't trust you."

"But I came back to—"

"We move on," Jack said. "Fleeter, I can't stop you coming with us. And I won't. But we're not going to sit and wait for whatever plans Reaper might have for us now. If we meet him, so be it. But we go."

"Yeah," Sparky said.

"Absolutely," Jenna said.

Rhali nodded her head. Even Andrew seemed to agree, his visage blurring with a half-smile.

"Lucy-Anne?" Jack asked.

"We go," she said. She looked at Hayden. He shrugged his backpack higher, and the tools inside rattled.

"Just get me to the bomb as quickly as you can," he said. "I'll do my best to do the rest."

Jack was curious as to exactly what had been used against the Superiors. He had little doubt that whatever it was had been developed from Miller's vivisection of those infected by Evolve, but whether it worked against the developing illness—or perhaps even caused it—was something that would have great impact in the future. Miller had said that the illness affecting many of those with talents was a side-effect of Evolve, but it could just as easily have been something Miller had created himself, whatever he claimed.

But the future where this would matter was far, far distant. The immediate future was less than four hours long. His injuries burned, eye throbbing, and he had yet to fully assess the damage done. But there was no time even for that.

As they approached the Imperial War Museum, Rhali used her gift to warn them of movement ahead. And there was plenty. Andrew also went ahead to scout their route, and he returned several times with tales of creatures wandering the streets. They were all heading in the same direction—towards the museum.

Jack sought ways to communicate with those things they would face. He did his best to think of them as human, although forcibly evolved far from what he understood human to be. But after everything he had seen, he also thought of them as monsters. Like Reaper, they looked down upon the Irregulars as way below them, insignificant as insects to an elephant. Unlike Reaper, they ate them.

His efforts frustrated him. His talents were many, but not endless. And search though he did, he could not perceive a way to touch those creatures from the north.

"We all want the same thing!" he said to Rhali. "They've come down here because of the bomb, though none of them can stop it. And even though perhaps we can, I just don't know how to tell them that."

"Can't you just talk to them?"

"You've seen some of what I've seen. I think they're beyond conversation."

Lucy-Anne had already shared with him what she knew of them from her time in the north. They looked wild, but carried a startling intelligence. They were vicious and brutal, but organised as well, sometimes hunting in packs for some of the scarcest food there was—humans.

Jack had asked what they ate in the north, and it had been Andrew who offered the answer. *I only saw it once but . . . think of farms where humans keep cattle. More than that, you don't want to know.*

And so close to the museum they called a halt again, hiding behind the innocent facade of a restaurant window, watching darkness fall outside and wondering what to do.

"Nomad is still inside?" Jack asked.

"She showed no sign of wishing to be anywhere else," Andrew replied. He seemed to flicker before Jack, like reality wavering in and out of focus.

"If she can get in, so can I," Jack said. "Maybe that *is* the first thing to do. I'll go inside, look at everything, try and find a way in for Hayden."

"But how can you get past everything Hayden says they have in there, even with your talents?"

"Nomad did."

"Nomad's almost a dream," Lucy-Anne said.

Jack's frustration was growing. Blessed or cursed with such powers, still he sat in an Indian restaurant where no one had eaten for two years, curled menus and neat place settings taunting him with the normality that was no more.

"Maybe Reaper had the right idea," he said quietly. "A distraction. Not for the Choppers, but for these things around the museum. Draw them away so that Hayden can get inside. Work on the traps. See what he can do. He's the tech guy, after all. Get into the tank and start dismantling the bomb."

"Me and Sparky," Jenna said.

"No," Jack said.

"But—"

"No! You'll be killed. They'll catch you easily. No, it has to be me and Fleeter. We're the distraction, you get Hayden inside, then I'll meet you back at the museum."

"You're taking on an awful lot yourself," Lucy-Anne said. "Why don't you let—"

"Where's Rhali?" Jenna asked.

As he stood from the chair he'd taken and moved to the front window, Jack already knew. *No*, he tried to say, but his mouth was suddenly dry.

He saw Rhali just as she disappeared around the junction at the end of the street, heading for the museum. *She's going to get herself killed!* he thought. But at the same time he realised that whatever happened when they pursued Rhali could be the distraction they needed. And she knew that.

"Fleeter!" Jack said, readying himself to flip and go to Rhali's aid.

And then all hell broke loose.

CHAPTER FOURTEEN
THREE

For a moment Jack thought something had happened to the sinking sun, shadowing the street outside and concealing everything from view. Then as the creature struck the window and smashed through, he realised what had happened. As they'd been sitting there talking they had been stalked. And now the stalker had closed for the kill.

He squeezed his eyes shut and crossed his arms before his face, yet still he felt the cool kiss of dozens of glass shards across his cheeks and chin, forearms and scalp. He backed quickly away and his legs struck a chair, sending him sprawling. Even before he struck the ground he was kicking back with his feet, trying to distance himself from the window and whatever was coming in, because it was big. It had to be to block out so much light.

Fleeter screamed.

Jack opened his eyes and felt the horrible tickle of shattered glass across his face. He looked at the floor and risked blinking rapidly, and his vision cleared.

Someone shouted. Jack lifted his head and picked up the chair at the same time, but the thing was paying him no attention. Its teeth and claws were concerned only with Fleeter. Its wings were folded around her, claws at their tips curled into her shoulders, and its bat-like face darted down again and again, biting chunks from her arms as she waved them frantically before her face. The creature had long blonde hair, and for what felt like several long seconds Jack became mesmerised by the flowery hair clip hanging from a few thin, filthy strands.

Fleeter's blood splashed his face.

His eyelids drooped and he delved inward, but Jack was not himself. He still felt a deep, penetrating pain from his face and eye wound that he had healed only so much . . . saw Rhali disappearing around the street corner and into danger . . . thought of his mother and Emily and whether he would ever see them again . . . and when he tried to send a freezing exhalation at the thing to still its sickening, gnashing mouth, his breath condensed before his face and fell to the floor in a fine snow.

Fleeter cried out, a single, desperate scream that chilled Jack to the core. *Everything is going wrong! Nothing is simple, nothing is safe, and I should be going after Rhali!*

From somewhere in the distance came the angry rattle of heavy gunfire.

Jack flipped, but without success. For a moment the scene around him slowed, but then staggered onwards like a film with frames removed. The bat-thing jarred and jerked, and other movement sent sharp shadows dancing across the restaurant's tables.

Shivering, feeling hopeless, trying to gather himself to use his powers as they were meant to be used, Jack could only watch as Sparky leapt across tabletops and powered into the bat monster, grasping its hair and pulling its head back, wrapping his legs around its torso and trapping its wings.

"Sparky!" he shouted. But Sparky was grimacing, his spiked hair spattered with Fleeter's blood from the creature's mouth as he brought up his knife and slashed it across the monster's throat.

It screeched and pulled back, launching itself back through the shattered window with strong, long legs. *Human legs*, Jack thought, and on one ankle he saw what might have been an Ironman tattoo. Sparky went with it, attacking with the knife and trying to get past one waving wing that the thing had worked free. It struck Sparky with it, and the sound of leathery wing against his head was like a palm against a brick wall.

Hayden was hunkered down beneath the window sill, whimpering.

"Help her and stay safe!" Jack shouted at him, pointing at Fleeter. He could see more blood than skin on the girl's face. But it was his friend who needed him most.

He heard more gunfire, and the sound of a helicopter coming closer.

Taking a deep breath and struggling to settle the turmoil of his talents, Jack leapt out through the window.

As Sparky jumped on the thing and started hacking with his knife, Lucy-Anne heard breaking glass from the kitchen at the rear of the restaurant.

If something gets in behind us . . . she thought, and Jenna obviously had the same idea. She tapped Lucy-Anne's arm and led the way back towards the kitchen doors. She glanced back only once, looking past Lucy-Anne at where Sparky fought the thing. Her eyes went wide. Then they were at the swing doors into the kitchen, and Lucy-Anne pushed them open first.

Weaponless, defenceless, she stormed into the kitchen.

The thing stood at the back of the large room, and for a moment she thought it was Shade. Right then she'd have welcomed him with open arms, even though he spooked the hell out of her. At least she mostly knew what he was.

But it was not Shade. And when the thing charged, Lucy-Anne had no idea what was about to kill them. It moved without sound, long limbs waving like fronds and lifting it over food preparation surfaces, body and head kept level and straight and focussed on them. It had dark, fluid eyes. Like a shark. And when it opened its mouth there were too many teeth.

Lucy-Anne darted left, ducking down and frantically scanning for something to use as a weapon. But it was Jenna who saved the day. She swept something from a work surface and hefted it at the advancing creature, and the meat tenderiser impacted its head with a dull thud.

It paused and shook its head, and in a shockingly human gesture it brought one long, delicate limb up to touch its face. It looked at its hand—long-fingered, thin, feather-like—and saw blood.

"Lucy-Anne, use *anything*!" Jenna said, and she started throwing other kitchen objects. Several glass jars, metal ladles, a wooden chopping board, some hit the thing on its head or dark, upright body, some were knocked aside by its thrashing arms.

Lucy-Anne moved along the side of the kitchen, pulling drawers open and heaving a handful of knives and forks at the creature. She knew that they had mere seconds. It might be surprised, perhaps even a little shocked at the sight of its own blood and the willingness of these people to defend themselves. But if it was as hungry as the other things they had met, and as dismissive of those still relatively normal, then in moments it would come. And bite.

She tripped over the body. It was shrivelled and dry, still dressed in kitchen whites that were now stained an autumn of browns. It rustled and whispered as she fell, and she kicked out in shock, feeling her foot pass through something dry and brittle. The head rolled. Hollow eyes turned to her. And then she saw the knife in the dead man's hand.

Jenna shouted, anger and fear feeding her voice. "Come on you bastard, stupid, stupid thing! You want to eat me? What would your mum say, eh? Would your dad be proud?" Lucy-Anne couldn't see her—the central food preparation area was in the way—but she heard the pots and pans, plates and glasses, cups and cutlery that she continued to throw at the thing, keeping it at bay. The shadows of its waving arms and stalking legs passed across the ceiling above Lucy-Anne as it lifted itself up to leap, and then she stood.

It was ready to pounce on Jenna. Had her in the corner, pressed against the closed walk-in fridge with nothing left with which to protect herself. But it was Jenna's wide-eyed glance past the thing at Lucy-Anne that saved her.

As the creature turned, Lucy-Anne jumped onto the work surface and leapt at it, dead man's knife sweeping around in her right hand. *Who were you?* she thought. *Who did you love, and are they still alive somewhere?* But she could not distract herself with thoughts of lost humanity. She was still human, and loved, and she loved others. That was why she was as prepared as any of them to kill.

It lifted one long arm to ward off the knife, but the keen blade had remained untouched by time. It sliced through the light limb and Lucy-Anne's weight drove it forward, burying the blade in the creature's neck. As the thing fell, she fell on top of it.

Its shriek of pain was the first sound they'd heard from it, and it was horrible. Lucy-Anne closed her eyes as she and the thing tumbled to the floor, and she could have been hearing a baby crying out in pain. But then it lurched her aside and fell across her, teeth gnashing, head butting at her even as she brought her left arm up to protect her face.

Jenna stumbled past and raised something in her hands, bringing it down on the back of the creature's head. Lucy-Anne twisted aside just in time, avoiding its head as it was driven down by the impact. She felt teeth grazing across her shoulder.

"Come on!" Jenna said, reaching for her. But Lucy-Anne could not try to escape from beneath the dying creature just yet. She held on to the knife and, with gritted teeth and eyes squeezed shut, twisted and shoved it deeper.

The thing that had once been a person shuddered, uttered a high-pitched keening sound, and then slumped down on her.

Jenna grabbed it and pulled, and Lucy-Anne pushed. She tried to close herself off from what she had done, dull her senses against the evidence of death. Warm blood, the stench of its breath, the sound of its hard skin against her own, the pain in her shoulder . . . she tried to ignore them all.

"Shitting hell," Jenna said. "Come on. Up. Thanks. Come on, Lucy-Anne."

They stood together in the kitchen and hugged, holding each other so tight and both trying to turn so that they could not see the dead thing. Lucy-Anne looked at the door through which it had entered, and there was no sign of any movement. But that route was open now, and she was not sure she could bring herself to kill again.

Its blood was already cooling on her hand and forearm.

"We've got to go," she said.

From outside in the restaurant, someone shouted. And from further away, gunfire.

"Gotta help the others!" Jenna said. She dashed through into the restaurant, stepping over the body that might remain here forever.

As she followed, Lucy-Anne was already recognising what was happening because she had seen it all before. The shooting, the chaos, the death, and now the screams.

Nomad is coming to kill me, she thought. But fate carried her onwards, and she rode its insistent wave.

Out in the street, gunfire and shouts. The shooting was from some way off—Jack knew it was coming closer, though he could not worry about it right then—and the shouting was from Sparky. He was tangled with the bat thing on the road. They'd rolled out between two parked cars and now fought on the central white line, Sparky slashing with the knife, the creature thrashing to try to buck him off. His shouting was senseless, wordless, exhalations of both rage and fear. If Sparky stopped shouting, he might actually think about what he was doing.

Jack glanced the way Rhali had disappeared, and he actually took three steps in that direction. But his friend was before him, fighting for his life. And back in the restaurant, it was Hayden whom they had to all protect with their lives.

He breathed deeply, gathered his thoughts, and reached out. "Sparky," he said.

Sparky glanced up and understood immediately, rolling aside, leaving his knife snagged in one of the thing's tattered wings.

Jack lifted it up. It rose from the road, untouched, and paused in its screeching and thrashing to look around in wonder. He didn't know what he was going to do with it. If he simply dropped it along the street it could well come at them again. Once again Jack thought, *If only I could communicate with it, maybe—*

Something dropped on him. It must have been up on the roof, waiting for an opportunity to leap down on some unsuspecting victim, and it crushed him down to the sidewalk. He lost his hold on the bat thing, fell, cracked his knee and elbow painfully, and as if drawn by pain the creature attacking him reached around and pressed its forearm across his wounded eye, pulling his head back and exposing his neck.

Jack threw his head back hard and felt it connect. The thing grunted and let him go, and Jack took the opportunity to stand and face it.

Beyond, the bat thing was running at Sparky once more.

The woman before him was naked and sleek, and she stank of gone-off fruit. Though not possessed of anything extra—no wings, or stings, or altered skin—still she was distinctly inhuman. Her head was elongated, her limbs too long and her body too thin, but it was her eyes that were most alien. They glimmered with an arrogant intelligence, as if she could see far more. And she looked *so* hungry.

Jack reached in and down, pleased at last at the clarity his universe had taken on once again.

Sparky screamed. Startled, Jack glanced across to see what could draw such a shocking noise from his friend, and then the woman was upon him again, knocking him back across a car bonnet. In an instinctive act he surged heat at her, and she groaned as the skin across her right shoulder and upper arm sizzled black. But still she came, falling on him and reaching for his face with both hands.

One finger scratched across his wounded eye. Jack gasped, writhed to dislodge her, punched at her without really seeing where she was. His fist connected with her teeth and he felt a surge of blood across his hand. His, and hers.

Sparky shouted again.

Jack tried to flip, but his universe was in chaos once again. Pain darkened it, and terror at what was happening—to Sparky, to Rhali, his other friends, and perhaps to Hayden as well—made him lose his way.

Gunfire, bullets, the rattle of lead hitting metal and the eruption of an explosion somewhere close by. Jack punched and kicked again but the strange woman was already gone.

A hand closed around his arm and hauled him upright. He blinked at the searing pain in his eye, closed it, and with his one good eye he saw Shade standing before him. He was more there than Jack had ever seen him, and he looked exhausted.

Behind him, Reaper. But this was a Reaper Jack had never seen before. Panting, sweating, eyes wide in desperation, his clothing awry and left arm held awkwardly across his body, desperation had almost taken him back to looking like Jack's father.

"You better still have him, boy," Reaper said.

At the far end of the street three Chopper motorcycles skidded around a corner. Above them the helicopter came in again, and its heavy machine gun started tearing the street apart.

Nomad's eyes opened and she cried out at the dream she was still having.

Lucy-Anne and blood and then there is no more air because . . .

She stood, cautious still of the bomb and its traps. Summoning every scrap of what she had, everything that had set her apart since Doomsday and still did now, she became less human than she ever had before.

And in the blink of an eye, she went to change the future.

Lucy-Anne stood in the smashed window and looked out at the street, and she had seen some of this before. It wasn't quite right . . . but even as she watched, events steered themselves towards what she knew was to come.

Reaper fell back as bullets ripped along the street. Jack was shoved across the car bonnet and fell onto the pavement, and the dark man who'd been holding him dropped behind the car. The vehicle jerked on its suspension as bullets stitched across the roof and windows exploded outwards.

"Jack!" Jenna called. She stood beside Lucy-Anne, eager to help but knowing that to do so would be suicide.

Can it get any worse? Lucy-Anne thought. She looked down beside her at Hayden cowering beneath the window sill. He was holding a blood-soaked handkerchief to Fleeter's face, and the girl's limbs were jerking and slapping the floor.

"Sparky!" Jenna shouted. She darted out into the street just as the helicopter passed overhead in a roar and a cloud of dust. It was so low that Lucy-Anne could see the pilot's eyes as he looked down, and she wondered what he saw. People? Or monsters?

There were both down here.

Sparky was lying across the other side of the street. He was on his back, one hand held up, one knee raised. His blond hair was now dark with blood. The thing attacking him had fled at the gunfire. Probably more sensible than they were.

Jenna was running towards him as the Chopper motorcycles powered along the street.

"Jenna, run!" Lucy-Anne shouted.

Reaper stood and turned towards the motorcycles. *Now he'll shout them to smithereens*, Lucy-Anne thought, but he held his chest as he roared, and the result was not as dramatic as she expected.

The lead motorcycle swerved, struck a parked van and flipped, spilling its rider and rolling past Reaper and the prone Sparky. It missed Jenna by inches and smashed against another vehicle, spinning on its side on the street and then bursting into flames. Spilled fuel flowed, carrying the fire wide.

The rider stood on shaky legs, one hand pressed to her side, the other tugging a pistol from a holster on her belt. As she lifted the weapon the air around her hazed and she seemed to crumple, skin glistening with frost. She coughed, and ice formed in the air before her. A tall Asian woman appeared from the shadows behind her and knocked her aside. She knelt beside the fallen Chopper, pressed her mouth across the struggling woman's mouth, and Lucy-Anne turned away.

The other two Choppers braked, turned, and powered back along the street.

Kill them! she thought, but Reaper was slowly bending over as if winded. Had he caught a bullet? She didn't know.

The helicopter opened up again and Shade screamed. He appeared from a shadow Lucy-Anne had not been aware of and stumbled across the street, both hands pressed to his guts, blinded by pain. Agony gave him form.

"Shade!" Reaper shouted, but the shadow man seemed not to hear. He staggered directly into the flaming pool of fuel, and his scream turned into a shriek.

Lucy-Anne dashed across to Jack. He was bleeding and holding one hand to his wounded eye. "Do something!" she shouted at Reaper, looking up at the helicopter cruising slowly towards them back along the street. Fire leapt from its machine guns. Bullets ricocheted.

"Lucy-Anne, got to get back . . . got to . . ." Jack said. He reached for her, staggered forwards, and she held out her hands for him.

From her right, the roar of motorcycles again. The rattle of small-arms fire.

Ahead of her, Jenna was kneeling by Sparky.

Along the street, Shade was screaming, stumbling, aflame, trying to reel in his spilling guts.

Now, she thought. *Now is when Nomad—*

Something smacked her in the face, knocked her head sideways.

As she tried to breathe and gargled only blood, she saw what she knew must come.

"No!" Jack shouted. "No, Lucy-Anne, no!" He couldn't quite understand what he had seen, how her face could have changed shape so quickly. She was still Lucy-Anne, but no longer the girl he had known.

The cool, logical part of him knew that she had been shot. But the pure emotional part of him that drove to the fore in this time of confusion and bullets, burning and blood, could not readily accept the truth.

She stumbled to the left, one hand coming up towards her face but never quite touching. Her pale skin was raw now, and her spiky hair was dulled by the colour contrast of her blood. Her eyes started to roll up in her head.

The rush of fury was terrifying. Jack's heart thudded in his chest, the heaviest impact, and his skin came alight, tempering his thoughts and sharpening his senses until he could see like a hawk, hear like a hound. What happened next was pure instinct, and yet he felt totally in control. For the first time ever, Jack and his new abilities worked completely in harmony. They flowed together, and were one.

As easy as breathing, he turned and pushed a heat wave along the street that peeled paint, melted glass, and ignited gas in fuel tanks. The two motorcycles erupted, enveloping their riders in flames, swerving and striking parked vehicles. Several cars and vans also exploded, and glass and twisted car body parts flew in a deadly flock across the road. One rider screamed, but not for long.

The helicopter pilot pulled up and tipped the aircraft away from the chaotic street. But not soon enough. Jack's shout caught it and brought it down, and it struck a roof and thrashed onto its side.

He closed his eyes and took in a deep breath. His tumultuous universe settled. He turned away from the crashing helicopter and the burning chaos along the street, and went to hold his friend.

But someone was there before him.

In a blink, everything changed. There was a *clap!* that reverberated through buildings and ground, and Jack's first thought was, *Everything has been renewed.* From the moment before the sound to the moment after, the potential of the future seemed to have shifted hugely, and he felt a moment of consuming elation that he had not experienced since before Doomsday. He could not explain it. And he did not try. So much was beyond explanation.

As Lucy-Anne slumped towards the ground, Nomad ran along the street. She leapt a burning motorcycle and ran at Lucy-Anne, grasped her as she fell, pushed her onto her back, and then she raised a hand above her head, middle and forefingers pointing.

What is she—? Jack thought, and then Nomad brought her fist down and punched a hole in Lucy-Anne's throat.

"What?" Jack whispered. His voice was a calm breath amongst the burning and crashing and the breaking of things.

Lucy-Anne arched her back and shuddered. Nomad raised her hand again, splashing blood across the road, blood also dripping from her hand. Lucy-Anne's blood.

Yet again, Jack's instinct took over.

And here she comes, Nomad, another movement in the chaotic street and yet the focus of everything. Flames lean away from her. She is the centre. She runs and jumps a burning motorcycle and her feet barely seems to touch the ground, and then she knocks Lucy-Anne down.

Lucy-Anne draws in a breath to scream, but blood floods into her lungs.

She tries to punch at Nomad, but her limbs do not obey her commands.

Pain rings in, but it is the ice-cool pain of trauma and shock. Her chest is heavy. She cannot breathe past whatever has happened to her face.

And then Nomad punches straightened fingers down at her throat, and Lucy-Anne feels the hot, painful rush of air into her lungs once more.

He saw Lucy-Anne shudder as a breath flooded in, and somewhere inside, somehow, he sensed the relief bleeding through her shock and pain. Other, more destructive powers reined in, and his skin tingled from his ears to the tips of his toes.

Nomad looked at him and almost smiled. Jack wondered what would have happened had he unleashed any of those powers. She looked weak and was bleeding from her nose and the corners of her eyes, yet she was still strange, almost alien, and removed from what was happening.

"Jack," a voice said. Jack frowned, but could not take his eyes off Nomad and Lucy-Anne. *Maybe she's dead anyway*, he thought, but he saw his friend moving as she struggled against the pain coursing in. She'd been shot in the face.

"Jack!"

Jack turned, and Reaper was behind him. "Not out of danger yet," the man who had been his father said. "And I . . ." He touched his throat, as if to signal what was wrong. Behind him stood Haru, blinking rapidly, seeming exhausted. For the first time Reaper looked weak, uncertain, as if something had been stripped away and he had been lessened. Was he scared? Jack wasn't sure about that. But he did see something in his father's eyes that gave him a moment of satisfaction in this terrible time—respect.

"Sparky?" Jack called. The boy was sitting against a shop front across the street now, Jenna beside him. He raised a hand and waved. *Bloody but alive*, Jack thought, and that was as good as he could hope for right now.

Fires crackled, glass broke, metal buckled. The street was a symphony of destruction. The helicopter was settling into the sagging roof of a jeweller's, lying on its side with rotors snapped off, fuel gushing down the shop's facade. Two Choppers had climbed from the wreck and were trying to crawl across the rooftop to an adjoining property.

Jack's heart sank, so quickly and deeply that sour sickness rose in his throat. *I've done it again*. He could see a burning corpse tangled with the wreckage of a motorcycle, and the stench was terrible. He looked at the climbing, scrambling Choppers and wondered who they were. There must have been more in the helicopter, dead or dying.

"I've done it again," he said aloud.

"She's . . ." Hayden said. He was climbing from the restaurant window, pale and shaking. "She's . . ."

"Fleeter?" Jack asked. Hayden nodded.

There was no sign of the evolved humans, creatures, monsters. Survival was their sharpest instinct.

It was becoming Jack's as well. Now that everything had gone bad, and people were dying, and he was killing again, survival was all that mattered. And Hayden was key to that.

"Come here," Jack said. "Quickly. Carefully." He reached out one hand.

Hayden started towards him, looking down at Lucy-Anne and Nomad, then at the ruins and wrecks of machines and people across the street. Shade burned and sizzled, no longer casting shadows. Now he was just another dead man.

"He's our hope," Jack said, nodding towards Hayden. He did not even glance back at Reaper to see if the man was listening. Jack knew it, and that was all that mattered. Everything rested in this man's hands.

"Jack," Reaper said, panicked, "quickly, I can't, I can't do it, but you have to look *now*!"

Lucy-Anne felt apart from herself. The unbearable pain was borne by someone else. She might have been dying. Nomad knelt beside her and she looked different somehow, less than what she used to be. She was bleeding.

I came here for you, Nomad said in her mind, but Lucy-Anne could not be sure whether the woman had really said it, or if she'd imagined those words.

Lucy-Anne tilted her head to the side and tried to scream at the agony, but she could make no sound. Her body was no longer hers; pain was its master now.

There, she thought, returning Hayden's gaze as he stared down at her in frank fascination. *There's our only hope. And I've never dreamed this far.*

And Hayden's shocked expression vanished in a haze of blood and bone as he danced to gunfire's tune.

"No!" Jack shouted.

Instinct—

He crouched and turned, reaching out and lifting the two surviving Choppers from the rooftop. Even as he was suspended in mid-air one of them swung his rifle, and Jack super-heated the weapon, melting it and the man's hand to a slick mess. The man screamed.

Jack heaved them over the rooftop and they disappeared beyond, falling and dying out of sight.

Jack dashed past Lucy-Anne and Nomad and knelt beside Hayden, reaching out ready to clasp and heal, hands heavy with powers he had only just begun to understand. But there was no healing these wounds. No powers on earth could gather these scattered brains, bring them together, make sense of them again. Their chance at stopping the bomb—their hope for the future—lay dead in a bloody mess across the road's surface.

Jack closed his eyes and searched, harder than he ever had before. But there was no trace of Hayden. He had been living and now he was dead, and there was no point in between from which Jack could gather any knowledge that might help.

It had all gone to shit.

The taint of pointless deaths forever staining his soul, he slumped down in the street, lost.

CHAPTER FIFTEEN
TWO

"They did something to us," Reaper said. "At the edge of London. Crossing the Exclusion Zone. They fired several artillery shells. I thought they were just bad shots, but then I smelled something, felt strange. Tired. It must have been some sort of gas to knock us out, but Haru froze the worst of it into ice. I didn't know what they'd done until I tried to . . . to shout." He was struggling to sound strong, as dismissive as he'd always been. But his fear was leaking through. Jack didn't think it was fear of death. He thought that Reaper was more scared of losing his destructive power for good and being normal again.

"They stole his shout," Haru said. "They stole my cold."

"Miller's last revenge?" Jenna suggested.

"He's dead?" Reaper asked.

"Yeah," Jack said. "The Choppers know what's happening, so when you went to them it was a gift. Their last chance to trap you Superiors so they still have someone to experiment on when everything's blown wide. And they wouldn't want such murderers breaking out of London."

"You'd call *me* a murderer, Jack?" Reaper asked, eyebrow raised.

But right then, Jack didn't care. So much had happened that he was finding it difficult to care about anything. He was withdrawn, distant from everyone and everything, prisoner of his own guilt and struggling to see light anywhere. The sun was down now, over London and in his mind. Darkness ruled.

Outside, something cried out in the night. He listened, but it was not human. Rhali was still lost.

"But you led them to us!" Jenna said. "Why the hell would you do that? Why would you think that was anything like a good idea?"

"We weren't sure they were following."

"Bullshit!" Jenna shouted. Reaper flinched, face stern. But he did not respond. "What, were you scared? When you found you couldn't shout someone apart? And are you so-called Superiors just the thickest crusts of dog shit on the shittiest covered shit-shoe in the history of shit? Are you? Huh? You've wiped out pretty much everyone who can do something about the bomb, and now we've got the last one here, you lead the Choppers right to us!" She looked ready to rage some more, but her fury seemed to wane as quickly as it had risen. She pointed at Lucy-Anne. "And look what happens." Her voice was suddenly lighter, sadder. "Just look."

Lucy-Anne was sleeping in the corner of the large room. It had been a nightclub of some sort at one point, probably turned into a drinking club soon before Doomsday. There were no bodies in here, but plenty of canned drinks and bottled water, and crisps and nuts. The main attraction, though, was its lack of windows. They were shut off in here. Jack wondered whether, if he really thought about it, he could cut himself off from everything that had happened outside.

But he could still smell the blood and feel the desperation of his friends.

He was tired. Sparky's wounds had been simple to tend to. He'd be scarred, but Jack had stopped the bleeding and knitted flesh where his two worst lacerations lay open to the bone. But Lucy-Anne's wound was far different. The bullet had passed clean through her face, but in doing so it had done major damage. Her lower jaw was broken, teeth smashed, cheekbones cracked. Her broken teeth had been driven into her throat, and if it hadn't been for Nomad opening an airway—a finger tracheotomy—Lucy-Anne would have suffocated.

As it was, Jack had eased her pain with a touch, but try as he might he'd not been able to reset the bones. Perhaps there were some who could. He had seen Rosemary's friend operate on Jenna to retrieve a bullet without opening her up. But right now, such damage was beyond his talents. She moaned, unconscious. Nomad slumped beside her, asleep herself. Nomad frightened Jack, because she gave off a heat and a stink that only he could sense. He thought she was dying, but she hadn't said a thing since they'd broken into the club. He'd moved close to her once to try to wake her up, but the heat and smell had driven him away.

The stench of death. And the heat, for all he knew, of hell.

"I was wrong," Reaper said.

"What?" Jack said, aghast.

"I was—"

"I heard what you said!" He could barely even look at the man. Frightening, powerful, inhuman, to hear him utter such words disturbed Jack as much as anything else. It made him realise how much was changing, and how useless everything had become.

"So now what?" Sparky said. "I mean, thanks for sorting me out, mate. And for Lucy-Anne . . . for doing as much as you can for her. But now what? Rhali's gone. Your charming dad's gang are mostly dead or gone. Apart from Mrs. Frost there. And Hayden's had his brains blown out."

"Yeah," Jack said. "I know all that."

"So you've got a plan?" Sparky said. "Cos we're shit out of time."

"No plan," Jack said. "Other than, just . . ." He shrugged, because what he was going to suggest was no plan at all.

"What?" Sparky asked. "Tell us. You sound like you've given up, and you *can't* sound like that. I won't let you."

"You saved us all back there," Jenna said, and she cut straight to the core of what was torturing Jack. Not the bomb, or Hayden's death, or even Rhali's disappearance. It was the fact that he had killed again that made everything seem so pointless. He knew it was stupid, but he couldn't alter the way he thought. Even if everything worked out fine, he had killed to make it happen. A world where that was the price was perhaps not a world worth saving.

"Maybe," Jack said. "Or perhaps I just made your pain go on a little longer."

"What, you wish we'd all been killed?" Jenna asked.

"Screw that," Sparky said. "And screw you. I'm going for the bomb even if you're not."

"Me too," Jenna said. She was sitting beside Sparky, grasping his hand tightly in hers as if she would never again let him go.

"I'm so scared of myself," Jack said. He looked at Nomad but she was still slumped beside Lucy-Anne, as if echoing the girl's state. He'd started to hate the woman for what she'd turned him into. His gifts should have brought only good, but instead he'd become a killer.

Just like his father.

"Are you scared of me?" he asked Reaper.

"I'm scared *for* you," Reaper replied. He looked like Jack's father, but that was because he was trying. Stripped of his power, he was using other means to advance whatever his cause might be. *Give him his powers again and he'll be as much a monster as ever*, Jack thought. He snorted and turned away.

Lucy-Anne was looking at him. He caught his breath and went to her, and when they saw she was awake the others gathered around as well. Sparky held Jack's arm and Jenna pressed close to him, and he had to fight back a sob. His friends were loyal, and close, and there was nothing he wouldn't do for them.

Nothing.

Giving up could never be an option.

Lucy-Anne was trying to speak, and Jack could see the pain it caused her. They'd dressed some of her wounds with napkins, and Jack had stopped the worst of the bleeding. But the structural damage to her face was appalling.

"Don't try to speak," Jenna said, but Lucy-Anne grabbed at her friend's jacket and squeezed tight, clenching her fist against the pain.

"Gu . . . idee . . ."

"Got an idea?" Jenna asked.

Lucy-Anne nodded.

"I'll get you a pencil and paper," Sparky said. "Hold on. Hold on!"

An idea. Jack and Lucy-Anne looked at each other, and he wished he could pluck the idea from her mind. Wished it was that easy.

Sparky returned.

As Lucy-Anne began to write her idea down, Jack was still dwelling on that thought.

Pluck the idea from her mind . . .

The pain was part of her dream, and in the strange places she wandered, no one knew what she was trying to say. The London of her dreamscape had a bland, washed-out look—all colour was bleached, the sky was a monotone grey, and the parks and avenues were filled with the memories of trees. People walked the streets, but their expressions were neutral. Even when Lucy-Anne tried speaking to them, they only broke into slight frowns. Children walked with parents without being naughty, or inquisitive, or children at all. The River Thames did not flow.

The only splash of colour and life was the woman she was following along the South Bank. *Nomad!* she tried shouting, but the woman did not seem to hear. Either that or Lucy-Anne's voice was not working, because she could not hear herself.

I was shot. I can see, but not smell or taste. I can feel and wish I couldn't. Some of this is true.

So she ran after Nomad instead, sprinting through her dream of a London that never was, and each footfall jarred up through her body and reminded her of the pain.

Nomad turned, smiled, and Lucy-Anne imagined them meeting and embracing and the bomb not exploding.

She approached Nomad and held out her arms, and the woman raised her eyebrows in surprise. They embraced. *I think this is something I can do, for a while*, Lucy-Anne said.

When she opened her eyes she was talking to herself, and that grey London was deserted. But it was still there. No heat blast, no mushroom cloud, and a future that might just be malleable, for a time at least.

Maybe for long enough.

"You really think you can do that?" Sparky asked.

"It's all we have," Jenna said quietly. She was looking at Lucy-Anne, smiling and nodding.

"But dream a nuclear explosion not happening?"

"What else would you do?" Jenna asked, not unkindly.

"Get the bomb onto a boat. Float it down the Thames. Into the North Sea, or something."

"In . . ." Jenna glanced at her watch. ". . . less than two hours?"

Sparky frowned. He had no answer.

"It's the *only* idea," Jack said. They all looked to him, Reaper included.

"Getting pretty bloody desperate here, mate," Sparky said, shaking his head.

"Yeah, we are," Jack said. "That's why Lucy-Anne's right." He looked around at all of them, and he had tears in his eyes. Sparky, feisty and hard, but with a good heart. Jenna, resourceful and kind. And Lucy-Anne, who might well have lost more than all of them, and who now might be dying.

"Nomad," Jack said, pushing hard into her mind to make sure she heard. She raised her head.

Lucy-Anne tensed, trying to lift herself up, and Jack thought that perhaps she already knew. But hopefully that would not matter.

Hopefully.

Jack closed his eyes and flipped, and when he opened them again his friends were all but frozen where they stood, sat or lay.

"Jack," Nomad said. She had flipped as well, just as he'd hoped.

"I won't let anyone else die for me," he said. He didn't say what else he was thinking; not yet.

"And I'll do anything I can to help you and Lucy-Anne."

Jack moved across to Lucy-Anne, careful not to touch anyone else in case he hurt them. Haru exuded cold even now. And Reaper was in his way, raised a couple of inches from his seat. In that last moment before Jack had flipped out, Reaper had perhaps seen that he was scheming, and he had gone to stand and try to have some part in Jack's plans. But he would not.

Jack paused before his father and stared at him. Like this, his features again resembled those of the man he had once loved, and still did. The memory of his father was rich and strong, because Jack had strived to keep such memories close for those two long, lonely years between Doomsday and now. And he only wished he could find it in his heart to feel forgiveness and grant his father another chance. That should be how this all ended; with redemption and hope.

But he could not.

He resisted the temptation to nudge Reaper aside and knelt carefully by Lucy-Anne.

"I think I know," Nomad said.

"And you'll not try to stop me?"

"Of course not. It means you and Lucy-Anne get out." Her expression did not change, and there was no way he could read what she was really thinking. But even flipped out, he did not have time for a long discussion.

And I'll help too, Andrew said. He emerged from shadows at the back of the club and drifted forward. Jack was surprised, but only for a moment. He'd been wondering where the ghost had gone, but had already guessed that he would not have abandoned his sister.

"She'll be all right," Jack said. "You need to get her out of London, to a hospital, and they'll be able to fix her."

"Probably," Andrew said. "But shouldn't I be helping you?"

"Nomad and I will be fine," Jack said. For a second he thought that Andrew could see the truth. But the ghost said nothing.

"I'll have to tell them," Jack said. "When I flip back and get ready to leave."

"We could just go," Nomad said.

"No." Jack shook his head but did not bother trying to explain. Nomad was showing how far from being human she had drifted. He didn't know how he would tell his friends what he was doing, but he supposed the words would come when they were needed.

Jack touched Lucy-Anne's forehead, so gently, and looked at her terrible wounds before closing his eyes. *They'll fix her*, he thought, but he could not be sure. Perhaps he was trying to feel better about not being able to fix her himself.

Still touching her feverish skin, Jack dropped into his vast universe of possibility. The red star of contagion still pulsed, signalling that he should approach, touch, and spread its news. He turned his back on it and steered away, paranoid that it could sense his true intentions. It felt like a sentient thing watching his actions. Maybe it was him ascribing intelligence to it, but he could not be certain enough to relax his caution. *It won't let me leave it alone*, he thought, a strange idea that haunted him for every moment he was here.

He travelled, dipping closer to the points of light and then away again, searching, seeking the talent that would echo Lucy-Anne's. But he could not find it. Hers was a naturally occurring ability, not one initiated by the external influence of Evolve. Perhaps her own universe was far different from his own.

And so Jack tried something else. Concentrating all his attention on one point, and always conscious of the feel of Lucy-Anne beneath his hand, he started to form a star.

Skeins of light surged across his vision. Heat and cold vied for supremacy, and such were their extremes that he could not discern a difference. Stronger swathes of light drifted in, and a swirling shape began to form before him. He was in a dream, and the shape took on the outline of a rapidly condensing star. Creation took place. Jack was its witness.

He bridged the void between himself and Lucy-Anne, creating a path between universes across which he willed every facet of her amazing power. The star grew with her potential, and for just a moment he peered into the mind of another. It was amazing, and humbling, and so different from his own that he drew back in surprise. And then the new star was complete, and his universe was alone once more.

Jack touched the star and felt himself swell with Lucy-Anne's miraculous ability.

He sat back and sighed. When he removed his hand from Lucy-Anne's face, the newfound sun faded quickly into the background starscape of his mind, settling as if it had always been there.

"You now have more than me," Nomad said. She did not sound jealous, or amazed. She was simply stating a fact.

Good, Jack thought. *I might need it.*

"We should go," he said. He took one more look around at his almost-motionless friends. Reaper was a little further out of his seat, and Jack would have to be ready for him when he flipped back to normality. But he was confident that he could handle Reaper. He only hoped he did not have to.

Without another word to Nomad he flipped back, and she followed him moments later.

Lucy-Anne cried out, a wordless sound so filled with despair that Jack almost regretted what he had done. Nomad was there, settled in her seat again and watching them all with interest.

Reaper stood.

"What have you done?" he asked.

"Nothing yet." Jack turned his back on the man, trying also to shut Nomad from his view. He wished it was only him and his friends here for this final moment. But that was a selfish thought, and one derived from a naive mind that could exist only in a world that was fair and reasonable.

Lucy-Anne was trying to sit up, pressing the impromptu dressings to her face with one hand and reaching for Jack with the other. Jenna and Sparky tried to hold her back.

Jenna was staring at Jack.

"What?" Sparky asked. "What is it? What did you do? You . . . flipped, then back again. Where've you been?"

"Nowhere but here," Jack said.

"Oh, Jack," Jenna said, and he was filled with admiration and love for his friend, because she knew him so well.

"What?" Sparky asked again, frustrated.

"You're too badly hurt," Jack said to Lucy-Anne. He knelt before her and held her reaching hand between his own. She was breathing heavily through a bloodied nose, her airways cleared now, the wound in her throat covered with a wadded napkin. Jack had been able to close that wound, at least.

"Oh," Sparky said. "So . . ."

"So Jack's going to do the dreaming," Jenna said.

Lucy-Anne shook her head, then slumped against Jenna when the action made her dizzy. She groaned again. Jack held her to him, stroking her hair and enjoying the warmth of her. He'd held her like this many times before, but never would again.

"So we'll have to arrange where to meet you," Sparky said. "And how to get out of London without them doing to us what they did to Reaper's lot."

"I won't be meeting you anywhere," Jack said.

"Huh?"

Jenna started crying.

"Oh, no," Sparky said. "No mate. Absolutely not. Not after everything. No way. Not if I have to pick you up and carry you myself."

"And I won't let you do that," Jack said. He moved closer to Sparky and hugged him close. "There are other reasons," he whispered in his friend's ear. He let him go and looked at Jenna. She met his gaze and wiped her eyes. He could see that she hated this, but also that she knew he was doing something important, and that she could never stop him.

He could not tell her right now, because Nomad was here. He only hoped they would work it out.

"You'd better move," he said.

"Jack—" Jenna began, but Jack held up one hand. If they started a long good-bye, he wasn't sure he'd be able to go through with any of this.

"Just . . . kiss Emily for me." He took a breath, thought of plenty more he wanted to say . . . and then flipped.

For one final moment before Nomad followed him through, he looked at the best friends of his life. Lucy-Anne looked wretched, but he hoped she would not bear any guilt for what was his own decision. She was damaged in many ways, but she was also a clever girl. She'd understand.

Jenna's tears glittered on her cheeks and her fluid eyes reflected Jack's image. She and Sparky had such a future together.

And Sparky, his big strong mate, so ready with a quip but so sensitive underneath. He might suffer the most over what was to come. But Jenna would tell him why. Jack was confident of that.

He'd told her enough for her to work out why.

Jack left the club without taking one final look at Reaper. He preferred to remember his father as he had been two years before, and he hoped he would have been proud.

Out in the silent, still streets he breathed in stale air and waited for Nomad to join him. She came moments later. Without a word they set off for the museum.

Perhaps she still believed this was not the end.

CHAPTER SIXTEEN
ONE

Jack had soothed some of her pain, but Lucy-Anne could still feel the damage done to her face, and her friends' expressions when they looked at her told her everything she needed to know.

But she did not care about that. Neither did she care about what Nomad had done to her, and why, though it showed once again that her dreams were ambiguous things.

She cared about Jack and what he had done. It had been her idea, and he had taken it away. Stolen it for himself. Lucy-Anne was the one who should have been in the museum with the bomb—her and Nomad—but now Andrew was with her again, and they were going to try to leave London at last.

Jack had been in her mind. He'd left a sense of himself behind, and it was an almost sensuous feeling, like the memory of a kiss or the promise of making love. She could not help feeling that she'd lost him again, but she would treasure what he had left behind. Maybe she could dream it afresh again and again.

"We can't just let him," Sparky said. "That's stupid! We can't just *let* him."

"He's already there," Jenna said. "Between one blink and the next, he's gone to the museum."

And he's already dreaming, Lucy-Anne thought. Jenna was looking at her, the saddest smile she'd ever seen on her friend's face. Lucy-Anne nodded gently, trying not to disturb her wounds. *Dreaming us safe.*

"Well, he's a fool," Reaper said, standing, turning to go, and then

Sparky was on him, knocking him to the ground and punching with fists and forearms. Lucy-Anne wanted to shout for Sparky but she could not, so she had to sit and watch.

Reaper shrugged him off and Sparky sprang up, pouncing again as soon as Reaper tried to stand. They rolled into a table and sent chairs spilling, glasses smashing to the floor, drinks cans adding their own hollow shouts to the fight.

Reaper growled. The ground vibrated, and Lucy-Anne groaned aloud, standing and staggering towards the fight. Jenna grabbed her arm and held her back.

Andrew appeared from the shadows and smiled at Lucy-Anne. "You're going to be safe," he said, voice carrying above the struggling boy and man.

Reaper shouted. A window cracked somewhere, a bottle shattered somewhere else. Sparky stood, panting, hands still fisted by his sides.

Reaper stood as well, but he did not shout again. He did not say a word. Lucy-Anne wasn't sure whether he was able to roar anymore, or whether he chose not to. But he sat down again and looked down at his hands, and the rosettes of blood dripping onto them from his bloodied nose.

"Your son is not a fool!" Sparky said. "Get it? D'you get that, you bloody superior dickhead?"

Reaper did not respond.

"He's as far from a fool as anyone I've ever known," Jenna said. "You know what he's doing, and why?"

"Trying to stop the bomb," Reaper said.

"That's only a part of it!" Jenna said.

Lucy-Anne frowned, confused. *Only part of it?*

"He's seen what Evolve can do," Jenna said. "The talents it gives; they're amazing, and deadly. Who knows if anyone will find a cure to the illness, even if the survivors are welcomed outside London? Who knows anything? But he's also seen the terrible things it can do, too. Like you, Reaper. His father, the man he loved and respected and looked up to. The man he waited two years to find, and who he talked about every single day of those two years. And when he found him, Evolve had turned him into a murdering bastard. Someone who thought he was special, and superior to everyone else. And *no one* is better than anyone else. Jack knows that. And what Nomad gave him—the ability to spread the infection, and give it to other people—he knows the world isn't ready for that. It wasn't ready when Nomad spread Evolve, and it isn't ready now. I asked him. I wanted him to give me something to help, but he refused. And I'm glad he refused, because now I know why. It's because he loves me."

Reaper was still looking at his hands. There was fresh blood on them now, and it was his own.

"He's the only one who *isn't* a fool," Jenna said. "And the best way to honour him is to survive."

"You're talking like he's already dead," Sparky said quietly.

"He is," Lucy-Anne said. It hurt to speak, but she had to make herself heard. "To us . . . he is." She was crying. The tears touched her wounds—those injuries that Jack had also touched to take away the terrible pain—and made them sting. She was glad.

"We're leaving," Jenna said to Reaper. "And because despite everything I think Jack still held out a spark of hope for you, I'm inviting you to come with us. To be who you were before, not who you've become."

Lucy-Anne expected Sparky to object, but he merely stood to one side, head bowed. Remembering his friend.

"Andrew . . ." Lucy-Anne said, and she pointed across the darkened room.

"I will guide you out," Andrew said. "I've been to the west, and hundreds are gathering there already. But we have to go now."

Leaving blood and tears behind, they left.

They headed west. It was almost eleven p.m., and London's silent streets were as haunting as ever. But with Andrew leading them, Lucy-Anne felt a flush of confidence. The fear was still present—she thought that she would always be afraid, and the dark places she'd seen would remain as shadowy echoes in her soul—but alongside was confidence that they would make it. They had to. They could not let Jack's sacrifice be in vain.

She walked with the help of her friends. Sometimes she seemed to float, as if the weakness and pain from her injuries caused a kind of delirium in her. Other times, she thought perhaps Jack had done something to help keep her going, for a time at least.

Close to the river, Andrew whispered a warning and they left the street, hiding down a narrow alleyway between tall buildings. Sparky and Jenna knelt before Lucy-Anne and soothed her, protecting her with their bodies. Every time they looked at her she saw her injuries reflected in their expressions. They couldn't help it. She was never once tempted to put her hands to her face.

She swallowed blood. It ran past the hole Nomad had punched in her throat, and each breath she took was thanks to that woman. But every bad thing that had happened to them all was also thanks to Nomad. Lucy-Anne didn't know what to think about her, so she tried not to think at all.

Something passed the end of the alley, and a dreadful smell wafted along to them. They looked at each other but did not speak. They had no wish to attract the attention of whatever could make such a stench.

Lucy-Anne did not notice the point at which Reaper and Haru

drifted away. They'd left the club with them and followed, hanging back a little and yet still obviously a part of their small group. No one had spoken to either of them, and they had remained silent. But when they crossed the river at Battersea, the Superiors were gone. No one commented. But Lucy-Anne was a little sad, because she'd harboured a vague hope that Reaper might redeem himself. Help them escape, show that he cared in some way. It was the least he could do for Jack.

Sparky kept looking at his watch, worried, but Andrew simply drifted on. They could not move any faster than they were.

They met the first of the people at West Kensington. Irregulars, they huddled down in a small park and watched them pass by.

"Come on!" Sparky called to them. "Hurry up! We've got 'til midnight." They did not emerge again, but Lucy-Anne hoped that they would follow.

There were more people in Chiswick, and here they met a group of people who directed them to Breezer. He was waiting for them outside a ruined pub, a table set on the pavement before him filled with canned drinks and crisps. He looked around for Jack, raised his eyebrows, but no one felt like telling him. Verbalising what was happening would have made it all so much worse, and they needed all their strength to get out of London.

"I waited for you," he said. "Hundreds have passed me already, on their way out. I gathered as many as I could, spread the word as far as possible. And I've seen some of those things, too. From the north. We won't be the only ones leaving London tonight."

Those monsters outside London, Lucy-Anne thought, shivering.

But she wondered how well even the Irregulars would fit in, and whether they would be allowed. She imagined fenced fields with hundreds of people wandering aimlessly inside, guarded by watchtowers and machine-gun nests. She pictured huge labs built in warehouses, and people strapped down while scientists in Chopper colours took their blood and cut them up, examining their muscles, their bones, their brains. She saw a dozen children in a metal storage container, dirty with their own filth and crying for parents who would never come.

But when she spoke of her fears, it was her dead brother Andrew who went some way to laying them to rest.

"The word is out," he said. "Your friend's sister and mother planted the seed, and there were so many ready to take it up."

"Yes," Sparky said. "We knew a lot of them. And so did Emily."

"Thousands have approached London," Andrew went on. "The military tried to stop them but couldn't. Press helicopters are barely being kept out of London's airspace. Camps have sprung up all around. The relatives of so many lost in London are there. Lots have come to find people who are already dust. But some of them . . . they'll recognise some of the people around us now. Mothers and sons, fathers and daughters, will be reunited soon, and no one will be able to keep them apart."

"They'll be registered," Jenna said, echoing some of Lucy-Anne's fears. But the girl seemed to hold more hope. "They'll have to be. And maybe they'll be kept in quarantine for a while. But when it's seen how ill so many Irregulars are, a cure will become the priority. And then after that, getting back to normal."

"Or as normal as anything will ever be again," Sparky said.

"There," Breezer said, pointing ahead. "We're close. I've already been this far, but came back to meet up with you all." They closed on Gunnersbury and the edges of the Exclusion Zone, and saw a haze of light in the distance. It lit the sky like the lights of a town, and aircraft buzzed to and fro within it.

"You?" Lucy-Anne asked Andrew. But she guessed she already knew the answer to that.

"I dreamed myself not dead for you, sis," he said. "And I've done everything I stayed behind to do. It's down to you now. Survive. Do incredible things with your life. Be amazing. I know you will be."

"Andrew?" she whispered, sad, resigned.

"Though I won't be there to see, think of me sometimes, won't you?"

Lucy-Anne nodded because she could not say anymore.

"Hey, er . . ." Sparky held out his hand, then lowered it again.

"Thanks," Jenna said. "You'll be . . . ?"

"Okay?" Andrew asked, smiling. "I'm already okay. No bomb can touch me." He turned back to Lucy-Anne. "I'll wait here for a while longer, just to watch you go." He drifted away from them, pausing beside a tumbled wall and becoming a part of the night.

With one last smile, Lucy-Anne turned her back on her dead brother and led the way.

Jack felt sad at Fleeter's death. He hadn't grown to actually like her, but she'd been interesting, and in her own selfish way she'd helped them more than once. He thought that deep down past the surface arrogance there had still been a little lost girl. He wished he'd asked her name.

They'd left her covered with a jacket, just another corpse in the mausoleum of London.

He was also mourning his lost father, a period of renewed grief that had lasted for two years. And he felt terrible about leaving his dear friends. But thinking too much about them might undo him, and jeopardise everything he was trying to do. He had a plan and he was determined to see it through, because if he did not then it would have all been for nothing. The pain, the suffering and death. He could not let that happen.

He *would* not.

So he did his best to leave that Jack of grief and sadness behind, and the one who approached the museum was a new, simpler Jack. A young man with a mission, shorn of thoughts that might distract. He had become a memory with a purpose.

The scenario awaiting them was strange and troubling, but he tried not to waste too much time to wonder. The things surrounding the museum—frozen in the moment where they sat, lay, ran, flew, crawled—were amazing and terrifying. Jack walked quickly past them. The air was heavy and still, but sometimes he still caught a whiff of animal scents, unnatural and unknown.

"Hurry," he said. Nomad had been falling behind, and he'd not wanted to risk a look back. He feared that acknowledging her slowness would give her the excuse to stop, and they had so much further to go.

"I . . ." Nomad said. "I think . . . coming from here, to help Lucy-Anne . . . I dug deep, used everything."

Jack had to stop then, and he turned to confront Nomad. He was shocked at the change that had come over her. Still ethereal and mysterious, she was tainted now with smears of blood from her nose and the corners of her eyes. She looked lessened. The blood made her seem more human. "You're Nomad. You're the First Vector, Angelina Walker, the cause of all this!"

Nomad nodded without any sign of regret. "Yes. But I am . . . weaker."

"Not now!" Jack said. "Come on. Come on, just a few more minutes, get me into—"

"You go," she said. Her eyes changed then, seeming to glaze

over with something darker. She staggered forwards, reaching for the museum's perimeter fence, but Jack caught her before she fell. "You go on. I can't stay like this. The illness . . . is in me as well. It has been for some time, but I've been denying it. Too late, Jack. But you're strong enough."

"No!" Jack said. "I need your help. I'm not as strong as you think." But he lied. Desperate, anxious to get inside, still he needed Nomad with him. But not only for her help. He needed her because he could not let her escape London. Not with what she had inside, that potential for contagion. He was ready to remain here to keep his own infection contained, so he could never let her go.

He checked the time, and wondered how accurate the timer on the bomb might be.

Without warning Nomad flipped back, and Jack had to follow. The world came to life around them. Movement, sound, smells, much of it unnatural and strange. Jack grabbed Nomad's arm and ran.

Through the gates into the museum grounds, and something came at them from the left. Jack raised a hand to halt it, but the shape skidded to a stop and backed off. Other creatures moved aside. Perhaps these amazing, wretched things were scared of Nomad. Maybe they perceived some kind of hope in their sudden arrival.

Or perhaps it was simply that they had already eaten.

Nomad ran with him, grunting at every footfall. She was more human than he had ever known her.

"The doors?" Jack asked.

"Safe," she said. "The traps begin inside."

Jack knew it was a terrible risk, but he used Reaper's power to grunt the doors open. They fell back, hinges twisted and lock shattered, and he and Nomad ran inside. He had no wish to give those creatures time to rethink, so he skidded on the marble floor, turned, and breathed a gush of white flame at the opened doors. Glass cracked and shattered in the inner vestibule walls, and the flames lit the area as bright as daytime.

Jack shoved forward with both hands, feeling his power surge through the air and catch the doors, slamming them against the darkness of London. He kept them closed and melted their hinges, twisting the lock back into place and melting it into one piece. It might not withstand a sustained assault. But it would have to do.

"Show me," he said to Nomad. She was staring at him with those glazed eyes, and he saw the respect and wonder. But he could not pander to that. "Show me!"

"This way," she said. He followed her into the main hall where machines of war stood on pristine plinths or hung from the ceiling. She held up a hand and they came to a halt. She pointed. In the darkness Jack saw the fine tendrils of lasers crisscrossing the large space, and the glimmer of trip wires. Then she touched his arm and pointed at the hulking shadow of a tank at the other end of the hall.

There, she said in his mind.

Jack could see that she was getting worse. That did not concern him now. It would help when the time came.

"We don't need to get too close," he said.

She was looking at him wide-eyed. "I've brought you as far as I can," she whispered. "I can't stay here, Jack. I know you must, and I won't change that. But what I have is too precious and it has to be preserved."

"No."

"Yes. It has to be spread."

"No! It's not precious. It's *poisonous*. And you're staying here with me."

Every scrap of her illness—the weakness, the blood, the distant glaze to her eyes—vanished in an instant. She seemed to expand as she took in one huge breath, and Jack wondered at the effort and energies it took to drive down that sickness.

"Nomad—" he began, but then she turned and ran for the doors.

He followed. The bomb behind, Nomad in front, both were terribly destructive, but Nomad was probably worse. The bomb could end London and all the history of that great character city. Nomad, and the contagion she carried, would change the world. Some of the change might be good, but the possibility was too great that much of it would be bad. In London she had been her own person, but out there in the wider world, she would be precious. Sought-after. Jack tried not to imagine Nomad weaponised. He tried not to imagine an army of a thousand Reapers.

She shoved at the doors and they flexed in their frames, creaking and breaking. Jack dipped into her mind and broke her link with the doors. She stumbled forward, as if a great barrier had been removed before her.

"You'd dare enter my mind?" she asked.

"Please listen to—"

Nomad shimmered and Jack flipped just as she did. He recovered from the familiar shock just in time to catch a fist to his face. A real flesh and blood fist, knuckles grinding across his nose and opening wounds that had only recently stopped bleeding.

He dulled the pain that melted into his skull, skipped through the universe she had planted within him, and then that red pulsing star of contagion seemed to expand and surge at him, seeking his touch and the gift of release. It exuded both vigour and sickness, and he veered away.

But it had given him an idea. Inside him was this alien thing, and inside Nomad there might be something similar. Or some*one*.

As Nomad smashed open the doors and they spilled to the floor, Jack knelt behind her and concentrated hard. She'd raised a much heavier barrier, but she still did not quite understand that everything she could do had also been given to him. He circled the barrier, observing, and then drove down and into it, hauling himself through. Before she could do anything he was drifting into her own universe of potential.

The shock at entering her mind almost froze him. Her place of talents was so different from his. It was colder, for a start. The stars more distant, the spaces in between so vast, more hollow, more empty. There was no personality to this place, and that made finding what he wanted that much easier.

He sought the personality she had once been.

Jack excavated. Unearthed the truth she had kept buried for so long. Freeing who she really was. He touched the star and let it burst, and its light flooded Nomad's subconscious. When he pulled out and drew back from her, readying for another attack, preparing to defend himself if what he'd tried went wrong, it was not only Nomad slumping to the ground before him.

Angelina Walker was a part of her once again.

She looked up at Jack with haunted eyes.

"You're staying with me," he said, and before she could react he stole her breath until she fainted away.

Jack used everything he had to venture closer to the tank. He mapped the trip wires and lasers in his mind, forming a three-dimensional understanding of where they were, and then sought out the other traps. He moulded a space of motionless air around motion detectors, levelled the temperature around body heat detectors. Paused by the inner doors, wondering what he might have missed and probing inside the tank with all of his human senses, and many senses that were far from human.

The bomb was in there, hot and heavy. The tank was welded shut.

"Angelina," he said. The woman was leaning against the wall beside him, eyelids fluttering, leg twitching. "Is there anything else?" He brought her up out of her faint.

She was scared, shivering, useless. She would be no threat to him as she was now, but neither could she help. This was all on him.

"We're going closer," he said. "I have to be as close as I can. Come with me."

Everything was still, and quiet, and as far removed from London as he had been in days. He stared at the terrible display of war machines, portraying both beauty in form, and ugliness in their intended purpose. Each one told a story now lost to the dark mists of long-finished wars. And yet each story still resonated, because Jack felt the influence of the people who had manned these machines. He had a duty to them as well as to everyone left alive in London. He had a duty to the world.

"What did you do?" he asked Angelina, not expecting an answer. But she gave one anyway.

"Only my best," she said.

"You can help me put everything right," Jack said. "I'll sleep, but I need waking every few minutes. You can do that. You have to."

Angelina nodded, and he saw no deception in her. He would have to trust her.

They moved closer until they were only a few feet from the tank, and then they stopped. They sat down slowly, Jack checking all the time for lasers he hadn't seen, pressure pads or trip wires hidden in shadows. But he knew that they were safe, for now. With the powers he had, he knew.

He could sense the bomb inside, a terrible weight. And he knew the time was close.

"Lucy-Anne dreamt of Nomad and the bomb," Jack said. "I have to do the same." He closed his eyes and started breathing deeply, falling into his universe and then passing through an unknown place into Nomad's stranger, cooler mind.

And he dreamt of Lucy-Anne.

CHAPTER SEVENTEEN
ZERO

"Shit," Sparky said. "Maybe they are going to machine-gun us after all."

They were halfway across the Exclusion Zone, and facing them was a wall of lights. They could see the movement even from here, hear the engines. Several helicopters buzzed overhead, but they couldn't tell whether they were military.

But they had already seen groups of people ahead of them disappearing into the bustle at the edge of the zone, and there was no gunfire. They had little choice. Lucy-Anne knew that Jack could not dream the bomb back forever.

"Time?" she asked through her damaged mouth.

Sparky glanced at his watch and kept staring for a while, as if trying to make sense of something. "It's almost midnight," he said.

"He'll do it," Jenna said. "For as long as he can, he'll do it."

Lucy-Anne had an arm around each of their shoulders, three friends so close. If only their fourth was not missing. She felt as though she'd left a limb behind, and several times crossing the bombed and burned Exclusion Zone she experienced a mad compulsion to rush back into London to be with Jack. She knew where he was. She might even get there in time.

"Almost there," Sparky said. "But don't these people know what's happening?"

"Maybe it won't reach this far," Jenna said.

"Yeah, but it's still close."

"Lots have left already," Breezer said. "I'm hoping this is the last of them. Others might have gone in different directions, but everyone my people were able to contact were told to come this way. There are some who refused to leave London. And probably many more we don't know about, deep down in the tunnels, hidden away."

"And those things from the north," Sparky said.

"Yes. And them. I've seen some . . . but not many. It could be many of them don't want to leave London."

"We can hope," Jenna said. "The thought of them out in the countryside . . ."

"I suspect they'll be as scared as we are," Breezer said, betraying his own fear at leaving the toxic city that had been home for two years.

"Let's go," Lucy-Anne said, wincing at the pain. It was her way of saying, *Shut up and let's get the hell out of here.*

As they approached the outer edge of the zone, the buzz of frantic activity was obvious. There was surprisingly little military, and those who were there seemed as panicked as everyone else. People rushed to and fro, calling names, searching for loved ones among the slow trickle of people emerging from the darkness of the Exclusion Zone. Cars and other vehicles were moving in only one direction—away. And those few still remaining sat with engines running, ready to leave as soon as possible.

These were the people of Britain come to rescue survivors they had been told were all dead. Until very recently this area would have been occupied only by Choppers, but now most of them were gone—obeying or against orders, Lucy-Anne did not know—fleeing the bomb that mad bastard Miller had triggered. Instead of waiting here until the last minute, helping the survivors get out, holding back the hundreds or thousands of people who had flooded towards London when the truth had emerged . . . they had turned tail and fled. Lucy-Anne had not thought she could ever hate the Choppers any more, but she did right then.

And though she loved these people who had come to help, she was also afraid that another tragedy was imminent.

"Buddy hell . . ." she muttered, and then a faint washed over her. She felt Sparky and Jenna strengthen their grip, and then everything drew far away. Blackness pulled her down, and she welcomed it.

He is walking along the South Bank. London is all but silent; the only sounds are litter blown by the breeze, and pigeons cooing in the trees. The London Eye is a smashed ruin behind him, but though wrecked it still feels like a special place. A place of creation and birth. Now he is leaving it behind.

He walks along the pavement but barely touches it. *I'm Nomad*, he thinks, and the sudden burst of lucid dreaming is a shock. It chills and excites him, because he has never felt its like before. He looks across the river and imagines one of the buildings there lifting up, and with a grind of breaking masonry it does so, huge columns of stone splashing into the Thames. He blinks and everything is back to normal.

It is amazing, but this is no time to play. Jack knows he has a job to do.

A voice calls out from behind him. His urge is to continue on and ignore it, but that is Nomad's dream, not his. So he turns around to see Lucy-Anne running along the riverside towards him. She looks petrified.

Any time now, Jack thinks.

Behind him, a flash. Lucy-Anne's eyes go wide and her face drops.

Now . . .

Jack dreams everything back to normal. The flash recedes almost before it begins, barely even glittering from the river's surface. The sky returns to its indifferent blue. Lucy-Anne no longer looks scared.

I did it! Jack thinks, and in the dream Lucy-Anne pauses close to him, looking around in confusion as if not knowing what to do.

"Don't worry," Jack says. He speaks with Nomad's voice. "I'll see you again."

Jack snapped awake. Angelina was beside him, shaking him gently. She moved back as he sat up.

"It worked," he said.

"For how long?"

He looked at the tank. It should have been blasted to atoms and beyond, but it remained whole because of him. "I don't know," he said.

"How will we *ever* know?"

Jack contemplated the moment of the explosion. He knew little about the workings of such a device, but he thought there was an initial charge that started the nuclear reaction. Would he hear that first blast? Would it reach his ears and travel to his brain, registering there before he was vaporised? Even with something as unimaginably destructive as this there had to be a moment between living and dead. An instant in time when consciousness ceased and his senses halted. He wondered whether at that instant, he would know what was happening.

Or would there be no knowledge? Would he be ended halfway through a thought or action, a movement or dream? Ceasing to be, like a raindrop touching an ocean.

He wasn't sure which would be best.

Jack was tempted to force the tank open, touch the bomb, start to dismantle it, look inside to see if there was a timer he could find, one which perhaps had been put back hours or minutes by the dream he'd just had. *I forced it to unexplode*. But he was afraid in case all of his powers could not combat the most subtle of booby traps.

And he was afraid in case he'd only put the timer back by seconds.

Lucy-Anne knew that voice.

"I can't go with you. You think they'll let me through? You think they'll let me live?"

"So what are you going to do?" Sparky asked.

"Haru and I will fade away."

"What about Emily and—" Jenna said.

"I haven't been her father for a long time."

"Thank you." That was another voice, and it took a while for Lucy-Anne to place it. She struggled to open her eyes, and when she did it was difficult to focus in the darkness.

"You're welcome," Reaper said. "Now . . ." He did not finish; perhaps because he had no idea what to say.

Lucy-Anne saw him then, Reaper, silhouetted against the flood-lights set along the edge of the Exclusion Zone. She couldn't make him out in detail—couldn't see his expression, his eyes—but when he walked away and disappeared into shadows, she thought perhaps his shoulders were curved, weighted down with everything he had done.

Or maybe he was just trying not to be seen.

"Where did he find you?" Sparky asked.

"Hiding in a basement," Rhali said. "He was calling for me. After I ran I was terrified, I got confused, so I headed west. Heard the shooting and explosions behind me and ran until I was exhausted. And I thought Reaper was going to kill me."

"Rhali," Lucy-Anne said.

Rhali knelt beside her and touched her leg, appraising her wounds without wincing away.

"But he came to save me. For Jack, he said. He saved me because I meant something to Jack. So . . . Jack?" Rhali asked.

Lucy-Anne shook her head.

"Is he . . . ?"

"Dreaming us safe," Jenna said. "Come on. We'll tell you on the way out."

They were outside London once again. Beyond the Toxic City. And everyone was on the move.

Vehicles screamed off into the night—cars, vans, buses, motorbikes, four wheel drives. Heavy lights illuminated the landscape for hundreds of feet in every direction. A score of coaches trundled along a road, two abreast, all of them jammed with passengers. Many more people walked.

They saw a wall of faces. On hoardings surrounding a church—its refurbishment abandoned two years ago—people had started pinning photographs and messages to lost loved ones. Someone had painted ragged letters across the top of the hoarding in an attempt to form some sort of alphabetical order, and many people frantically searched the images or sat at the wall's foot, waiting for a miracle.

"One minute," Rhali said. "Just one!" She ran to the M section of the wall and started looking. Searching for her own face, or a message from someone she loved. *No hope*, Lucy-Anne thought. She felt emptied by all that had happened, and any dregs of hope she retained were kept for Jack, and Jack alone. She had none to spare.

But then Rhali froze, reached up, stood on tiptoes. Everything seemed to pause as they saw her touch her own smiling face—happier from years before, fuller—and then pull off a square of paper attached to it.

She returned to them, stunned. "My cousin," she said. "My cousin Jay has been here. Looking for me. And he left . . ." She held out the paper, unable to say any more. Lucy-Anne saw some phone numbers, and a big *Jay* followed by an even larger *X* as a kiss.

"Whoa," Sparky said.

"Let's go," Rhali said, smiling. "He'll be waiting for me to call."

There were a few groups of people hugging deliriously, seemingly ignorant of the panicked retreat from what was about to happen in the city. Those lucky few who had met those loved ones come to find them. Lucy-Anne wondered what powers these people had, and what those they loved would think of them. How they would integrate back into normal, real life hardly bore thinking about. What would Jay think of Rhali now?

But that was not Lucy-Anne's problem. She had her own to contend with. These terrible injuries. Her dreams.

"What'll we tell Emily?" she asked as they walked.

"We'll tell her how brave her brother is," Jenna said. "How proud of her he is. Look at what she's done! She's revealed the truth to the world. If it wasn't for her, all these people might well have been shot down as they tried to leave."

"And we'll tell her her daddy's dead," Sparky said.

Lucy-Anne was shocked for a moment, remembering Reaper slinking away into the shadows after bringing Rhali back to them. But after everything he'd done—and she had only seen and heard about a fraction of it—that was nowhere near redemption.

No one objected to Sparky's suggestion.

"Where do you think we'll find them?" Jenna asked.

"Knowing Emily, it wouldn't surprise me if they found us," Sparky said.

Lucy-Anne looked back across the bombed Exclusion Zone

towards the distant, dark London. There were no lights over there, and the starlight gave only a surface silvery sheen to what she could see of the city.

She knew that however strong Jack's dreaming, the darkness could not last all night.

He sees Lucy-Anne again. It is a beautiful moment, even though he knows it is only him benefiting from the sighting. This is Nomad's dream he is redreaming, and retelling, after all.

He has a second to dwell on her beauty. Not only on the outside, because her rebellious, perky attractiveness has always been obvious to him. But on the inside as well. She has lost so much, but even so she did not allow the madness to carry her away. It stole her for a time. But she triumphed.

And then the flash behind him. London is bleached, as if the explosion's power is already erasing the city before its heat and shock blasts can do the real work. The skin on the back of his neck stretches.

Lucy-Anne's eyes go wide and her face drops. And then he sees her eyeballs melt as—

He dreams it all back to normal. He dreams it . . . back . . . to normal.

London displays its true colours again, and the pigeons in the trees coo plaintively.

Across the Thames, a building is burning.

Lucy-Anne raises her hands to her face, and as the scream forms in her throat—

Jack woke up. Shook his head. Pushed away Angelina's hands as they flapped at his face, holding one cheek and slapping the other.

"Not long," he said. "I can't do it for long. Maybe Lucy-Anne could have. I'm sure she could. But I . . ."

The tank's bodywork seemed to vibrate, filled with barely restrained energy.

"Maybe next time," Jack said.

"It's not fair," Angelina said. She was crying.

Jack could find nothing to say to her, so he leaned back and closed his eyes, thinking of his friends.

CHAPTER EIGHTEEN
MINUS ONE

They hitched a ride with a family in a camper van. There was a man, a woman, and a young boy. They'd come to find their daughter, but there had been no sign of her.

"Did you see Annabelle?" the desperate mother asked. "Seventeen, blonde hair, denim jacket? We've thought she was dead all this time, ever since Doomsday, but now we hear about all this . . . all these lies . . . and we came to find her. Do you know her? Did you see her?"

Everyone shook their heads, and Lucy-Anne was glad for her wounds, because she could not say what she was thinking. *She's probably dead, buried in a mass grave somewhere. Or if she did survive Doomsday, she might have developed an amazing power. In which case she's likely dying from the illness Evolve also gave everyone. Or she might be a murdering Superior. Or maybe the Choppers dissected her to see what made her tick. So no, we haven't seen your daughter. Concentrate on your son.*

The family were very kind to them, giving them food and drink they'd brought along in their camper van, and they volunteered to take them to a hospital. The hospitals were already overflowing with people who'd come out of London, they said, and they had a long way to go before they gave up on their little girl.

In this family's outlook, Lucy-Anne found hope. They seemed so accepting of the people who'd emerged from London after so long. They spoke of a huge charity push that was being organised, led by a core of movie stars, musicians and actors, and which aimed to raise a hundred million pounds in the first year for rehabilitation and treatment of London's survivors.

They spoke of the government, and how the Prime Minister had already stepped down. Foreign reaction, and how other countries were being accused of complicity. The mood of the general populace now that the truth was out. The people had been deceived and fooled by those in charge, and never had the gulf between ruled and rulers been so wide and deep. "There'll be chaos for a while," the man said. "The likes of which Britain hasn't seen before. But there's a real pulling together of people at the moment. It's the people who were lied to. It's us who are going to make things change."

They spoke a lot more, but Lucy-Anne drifted in and out of consciousness.

And she dreamed.

She runs along the South Bank and sees Nomad before her. Calls her name. Nomad turns, and smiles, and then it is not Nomad at all, but Jack smiling back at her. She can see the pain in his eyes, both the good and the bad one, because his injuries are apparent in the dream. As is his tiredness, and his strain. His smile is pure and unforced, but Lucy-Anne can tell that it is taking every ounce of physical and mental strength for him to hold the dream together, in peace.

She smiles back, her expression conveying so much. She tells him that they are safe and he can let go now. He can let go.

And then there is light.

Lucy-Anne jerked awake, breathing hard, gasping for breath. "Bad dream!" she said. "I had such a bad—"

But then she realised that she could see everyone's faces, even though it was the dead of night. And they were all looking back the way they'd come.

A false dawn rose over London as the city became truly toxic.

***

"We're safe," Lucy-Anne says. "Jack, you can let go now."

He smiles. Relaxes.

Light and heat sear across London, and as Jack starts seeing paint singeing and flaking on the ruin of the London Eye, he closes his own eyes.

He plunges into his huge universe of potential, a place filled with endless possibilities of human evolution plumbed far too early. He floats for a while, content. The red star of contagion no longer pulses for release.

As the points of light begin to grow, the red shifts to white.

And each star explodes, continuing to expand until they banish the darkness and join forever in one incredibly bright, cleansing light.

ABOUT THE AUTHOR

TIM LEBBON is a *New York Times*–bestselling writer from South Wales. He's had almost thirty novels published to date, as well as dozens of novellas and hundreds of short stories. His most recent releases include *Star Wars: Into the Void (Dawn of the Jedi)* from Del Rey, *Coldbrook* from Arrow/Hammer, the Toxic City trilogy from Pyr in the United States, and *Nothing as it Seems* from PS Publishing, as well as The Secret Journeys of Jack London series (coauthored with Christopher Golden). He has won four British Fantasy Awards, a Bram Stoker Award, and a Scribe Award, and has been a finalist for International Horror Guild, Shirley Jackson, and World Fantasy Awards.

ABC Network is currently developing the Toxic City trilogy as a TV series, and 20th Century Fox acquired film rights to The Secret Journeys of Jack London series, for which Tim and Chris Golden wrote the first-draft screenplay. He is working on new novels and screenplays.

Find out more about Tim at his website, www.timlebbon.net.